DROW TRIUMPHANT

DROW TRIUMPHANT

ALISON BROWNSTONE™ BOOK FIFTEEN

JUDITH BERENS   MARTHA CARR   MICHAEL ANDERLE

DISRUPTIVE IMAGINATION

LMBPN Publishing
PMB 196, 2540 South Maryland Pkwy
Las Vegas, NV 89109

First US edition, January, 2020
Version 1.02, February 2020
eBook ISBN: 978-1-64202-684-9
Print ISBN: 978-1-64202-685-6

THE DROW TRIUMPHANT TEAM

Thanks to the JIT Readers

Dave Hicks
Peter Manis
Kathleen Fettig
John Ashmore
Diane L. Smith
Jeff Eaton
Dorothy Lloyd
Daniel Weigert
John Raisor
Deb Mader
Shari Regan
Jeff Goode
Paul Westman

If we've missed anyone, please let us know!

Editor
SkyHunter Editing Team

DEDICATIONS

From Martha

To everyone who still believes in magic
and all the possibilities that holds.
To all the readers who make this
entire ride so much fun.
And to my son, Louie and so many wonderful friends who
remind me all the time of what
really matters and how wonderful
life can be in any given moment.

From Michael

To Family, Friends and
Those Who Love
To Read.
May We All Enjoy Grace
To Live The Life We Are
Called.

CHAPTER ONE

Thick droplets of rain fell continuously and the water added to the oily puddles that filled the alley and drenched stray cardboard boxes left outside the few doors that opened into the narrow space. Alison chuckled and shook her head. One truth stood out that afternoon, and it brought a question with it. Why did she inevitably have to lurk in dirty back alleys for so many of her jobs?

I have a college degree and went to a prestigious magical high school, yet I spend half my time fighting thugs. I might as well have stayed a bounty hunter.

Hana stood a few yards away. She leaned lazily against a cement wall, her arms folded. Her long *tachi* rested in its sheath and despite her yawn, the huge weapon proved she wasn't there to relax. She was surprised the fox hadn't selected a hot-pink sword belt, especially given the long pink overcoat she wore. It didn't scream security or stealth but complaining about that lack was pointless given the plan for the job. Besides, once the woman foxed out, she wouldn't be able to hide anyway.

Everything should have been easy. It was supposed to be a simple job to protect an otherwise unremarkable businessman who was worried that he was in danger following trouble in the recent past. Things had turned complicated when the Drow's informants advised her that the businessman had been targeted by a group of wizard assassins because of his acquisition of an artifact at auction. She'd already tried to put the word out on the street that they should back off, but no one had sent a response via any of her underworld contacts. She had to assume the assassins hadn't given up. There was nothing more annoying than a man who took his job seriously, especially when he was a paid killer.

"Status report, Tahir," she ordered.

"There are a few more possible assassins en route to the target location," he responded through the small receiver in her ear. "You have time, though. They don't seem in much of a hurry."

"That means they think they can eliminate him, whether he's on the move or at his home. But they're still in the same place?"

"Yes," the infomancer responded.

"Then our decoy worked," she commented with satisfaction.

"It would appear so."

Hana pushed away from the wall. She craned her neck upward, a bright smile on her face as rain pelted her face and matted her long dark hair. "There's something so satisfying about rain. It always makes me happy, even when it's wet and cold."

"You live in the right town if you like wet and cold

rain," Alison muttered. She raised her hand and a small shield formed to protect her from the steady drops. "LA's much drier than here. It's been a while since I lived there, but it still feels like the most natural climate. Admittedly, Seattle has its share of cool things, but I don't think rain is one of them."

"Hey, come on. You need to think about it. Rain rules."

"How does rain rule?"

They'd been friends for a long time, but she still had trouble following the woman's train of thought at times. She reminded herself that was a good thing. Thinking too much like the nine-tailed fox might be distracting in most circumstances.

"Think it through. Water is life, right?" Hana winked. "At least for us. It's not like we're an Oriceran rock race." She spun, her arms outstretched. "And there's nothing like being in all this life."

"Most people in town simply call it getting wet rather than being in all this life."

Her companion simply smiled and continued to twirl. "That's because they don't think about it the right way. It doesn't matter how many fancy buildings they build in this city, as long as it rains, you know this is a living place and that makes me happy."

"Don't ever move to a desert city," Alison suggested. "You'll probably shrivel up and die."

Hana offered her a toothy grin. "I'd probably end up all leathery." She tilted her head from side to side a few times, her brow furrowed in concentration. "I wonder how easily magic can fix something like that."

"You'd be surprised," her boss replied. "Not every witch or wizard out there is a naturally beautiful specimen."

Her thoughts drifted to her time at the School of Necessary Magic. Many of her teachers didn't look as old as they were, but they still showed some signs of their age. Magic wasn't a ticket to immortality. Even King Oriceran would die of old age someday.

This is the problem with rain. It makes me think more than usual.

She fluffed her red jacket before she zipped it. "At least we don't have to deal with cactuses in Seattle."

Hana regarded her with mock indignation. "Cactuses are cute. And tumbleweeds."

Alison laughed. "Just because something's a desert city doesn't mean it's an Old West town."

"Sugimoto the cowgirl!" The woman mimed riding a horse.

"I don't think Las Vegas, as an example, is filled with cowgirls."

The fox grinned. "I'd make a good showgirl." She pointed to her head. "I could wear the hat too."

"Sometimes, I can't tell if you're serious or not."

"Good. It's more fun that way." Hana winked. "But enough about me being sexy on stage. Have you talked to Izzie about her favorite wolf lately?"

"Huh?" She stared at her friend in surprise. "Izzie? What does any of what we were talking about have to do with Izzie?"

How did we get from rain to Hana as a showgirl in a cowboy hat to Izzie? I'll get mental whiplash from this conversation.

"This is how things work." Her companion shook a finger. "You started it. You can't back down now."

She shook her head. "I started what exactly? You lost me a few sentences ago. Izzie's not a huge fan of cactuses or cowgirl hats."

"No, no. Not cowboy stuff or deserts."

"Then what? I'm not lying, Hana. I'm lost."

"Marriage. Duh. Isn't it obvious?" The woman scoffed and rolled her eyes.

"Uh…clue me in," she replied.

Hana pointed at her. "You got married and so now, all your friends around your age will start thinking about it too, eyeing their boyfriend and imagining the possibilities. It's like a disease—a plague."

Alison stared at her friend. "Marriage is a plague?"

The fox shrugged. "A nice one."

"And so I've passed the plague to Izzie?"

"Exactly." She nodded her head and clapped once. "Izzie's been hot for Luke since they were in school together, right? If it wasn't for all that dark wizard crap, they might have ended up together."

"I guess. Who knows?" She shrugged. The aforementioned incidents had also altered her love life, but she wouldn't give the other woman anything to chew on by daring to mention that. The past didn't matter. She had married the man she loved.

"It wouldn't be a big surprise if she went for it soon," Hana explained, "especially since she basically had no life for so many years. Why wait around when the people who ruined her life have finally been defeated? I'm sure she stares at Luke, trying to will him to ask her, and from what you said, he totally carried a torch for her all those years she was hiding from the Seventh Order."

How much of this is about Izzie and how much is this merely Hana wanting to talk about marriage without complaining about Tahir not picking up on her hints?

Alison sighed. The rain increased as if it could sense her mood. It slid off her spell, which effectively left her in a circular curtain of rain.

Hana licked her lips, her face alight with excitement. "I wouldn't wait around if I were her. That's all I'm saying."

"Whatever Izzie might do," the Drow began carefully, "it won't be for a while. Not only does she have to work out her feelings about her life and Luke, but she's always worried about her parents. From what she told me, the government called them back to Austin for some reason, and that has to weigh on her. She might even end up getting involved."

Her companion remained where she was and spread her arms to welcome the rain. "So? Her mother is the original bounty hunter and her father's the Fixer. And they have that little Cheeto-eater with them too. I bet there isn't much they can't handle together. They were kicking dark wizard ass when we were still sucking on our thumbs and wetting our beds."

Alison ran her hand through the water her spell displaced. Hana was right. There was a certain hypnotic beauty to rain.

"Sure, you say that, but imagine if the government called my dad to request that he handle something right away. It would mean something serious is going on. Painfully serious."

"Okay, so they won't get married like next week." The fox twirled again. "That doesn't mean she'll wait years and years. Time's more precious to her." She stopped her motion and lowered her head slowly. "Does the government really do that? Call your dad and be, like, 'We need you James Brownstone. You're our only hope! And then he's, like, 'To the Barbecue Mobile!'"

"The F-350 isn't called the barbecue mobile," she insisted.

"It should be." Hana stuck her bottom lip out in a pout. "Suggest that to him next time. I'm sure he'll totally start calling it that."

"Maybe." She scoffed. "And, yes, on occasion, they do request his help, but at least the government doesn't treat Izzie's dad like they expect him to go rogue and blow up half the planet someday. That's the crap side of all this. They defended him from the Alliance but they still don't fully trust him."

"No offense—and I'm a huge James Brownstone fan—but...you know, the Battle of Los Angeles." Hana shrugged. "Just saying. Your dad's career kind of puts your collateral damage in perspective."

"He's retired now."

The woman grinned. "Yet he keeps stumbling into trouble."

"That's not his fault. People merely don't know when to leave him the hell alone."

"True." Her friend gasped and rushed over to her. She tried to slap her hands on her shoulders but the shield prevented it and she jerked her hands away dramatically. "I had an epiphany. It's genius."

"This isn't another idea about that half-off leggings sale, is it? I don't think you'll be able to convince them to give you 'buy two get five free' without charming them."

Hana giggled. "No, not that. I don't need to charm people for cheap leggings anymore, and it's not about my wardrobe and sexy legs and ass. It's about your ass-kicking father." She lowered her arms and nodded sagely. "And your little Drow problem. He's, like, the most obvious solution in the world."

"We've talked about this."

"But I have a totally new perspective to share."

Alison narrowed her eyes. "You'll tell me to deliberately get him involved?" She shook her head. "This isn't like it was with the challenge. It's different this time, especially now that Miar and Novati are dead. I need to stick to having Drow solve Drow problems if I don't want this to blow up into something much worse."

The fox rolled her eyes so hard Alison wouldn't have been surprised if they fell out. "You're half-Drow, and Daddy Brownstone's involvement is already baked into this messed-up cake. You've used it yourself as a reason why you even have to get involved."

"What are you talking about?"

Hana lowered her voice in her best imitation of Alison. "Dad defeated Laena and that messed everything up. So it's my responsibility to fix it because I'm Broody McBrownstone and I have to solve all problems by myself or they'll kick me out of the League of Brooding Heroes."

League of Brooding Heroes? I'm much better...lately.

She scoffed. "I don't sound like that." She sighed. "Do I?"

"Don't make me have Tahir play a recording back." The

8

woman shrugged. "See? If he was responsible for messing everything up when he delivered his patented Brownstone Beatdown to the old queen, he can help you fix the situation by doing what he does best—breaking more things. You can't make an omelet without breaking a few eggs, right? You need more than one egg for a good omelet, so get him involved. No matter what happens, he'll always be a part of it, even if indirectly. If you have a nuke, why not wave it around a little? It stopped World War III from happening and this time, the nuke can be reasoned with or bribed with sauced meat."

"World War III hasn't happened *yet*."

Hana stuck her tongue out. "Jeez. You're taking the whole glass-half-empty syndrome to a new level."

"It's time," Tahir declared. "All the wizards have gathered. They've given no indication that they know they're being watched."

The fox stepped back and her smile faded. Her claws extended, and her eyes turned slitted and yellow. Nine glowing tails erupted behind her and swayed in the rain. "I used to be such a nice little fox. I charmed a few people here and there." She patted the hilt of her sword. "And now, I carry artifacts and weapons like this around." She tapped her ring a few times before her skin turned red. "Not that kicking criminal ass isn't fun in its own way."

"I'm glad to hear it." Her boss layered a shield over herself. "We're a security firm, not a negotiation firm. I'll open the portal now. Head through the second it's big enough. My hope is that a little shock and awe will convince these guys they've already lost."

Hana saluted her. "Through the breach, fearless leader."

Alison took a deep breath, raised her arms, and murmured rapid incantations under her breath while she also compressed flows of magic. Knowing she was capable of the spell was helpful, but she still needed practice before she fully mastered her new technique. She'd come a long way in a short time, though, which was encouraging. A small dot appeared in the alley and expanded to a full portal after a few seconds. What she'd first unlocked in anger, she could now execute more calmly.

I wish Myna were around to see this. Shit. I wish she were around to see everything. I kept telling her I didn't want any part of the Drow succession struggle and I'm knee-deep in it. But now, it's time to kick wizard ass.

The fox leapt through the portal and she followed immediately. They emerged halfway across the city in yet another dank alley boxed in by two tall brick buildings. The negotiating firm idea had grown in appeal. They would probably have discussions in a comfortable conference room rather than backstreets. At least it wasn't raining in that part of town.

The Drow dropped her makeshift umbrella spell and summoned a shadow blade. The portal closed behind her. It was time to negotiate in a different way.

The two Brownstone Security women stood behind a group of five wizards. The men all already had their wands out. They spun to face the new arrivals and their faces all mirrored wide-eyed disbelief.

"No, no, no," a tall bearded man shouted. His fingers tightened around his wand. "You can't portal. Everyone knows you can't. You can fly and you have the helicopter, but you can't portal."

Hana threw her arms to the side and made jazz hands. "Surprise, assholes! You're guest stars on the Brownstone Beatdown show."

Alison pointed her shadow blade at the wizard. "Yeah, surprise. This is the part where you're reasonable and you simply surrender because you totally fell for my little plan."

The bearded wizard's lip curled in a sneer. "I thought it was a little too easy."

"This doesn't have to be a big issue. I don't even care about taking you in. I'm not a cop and I don't need your bounties. You could merely agree to go home and not do something stupid. You might need to agree to share a few little biographical details, though, so I can keep you honest."

He glared at her. "Do you really think we can do that? Do you know who we are?"

She sighed. "I think you've been totally surprised by me and I've not heard anything to suggest you're remotely on my partner's level, let alone my level." She pointed to Hana and then herself. "And I think you can see there are two of us here, which means the rest of my team is still guarding my client. On top of that, your big plan to mislead us with your little fake assassins failed and we actually turned it around on you. So, I'll give you this one last opportunity to surrender or run away or whatever with a few little spells, like I said, to keep you honest. But there's no way you'll reach my client today and probably no way you'll escape this alley if you're stupid."

The wizard sighed and shook his head. He pointed his wand at the ground. His cronies frowned and did the same.

That's a good sign. I think? Time to roll with it.

Alison smiled. "Good. So you can be reasonable. It's rare in my line of work, but I do appreciate it when I see it."

"No, you don't understand, Dark Princess." He stepped back. "I appreciate the offer and I also understand that you have a duty to your client to protect them, but I have a duty as well. I take great pride in my work, and I'd rather die than fail to complete a contract I've sworn to finish. I would be an embarrassment, otherwise."

She frowned. "Uh...your contract involves killing someone for money. We're not exactly talking the stuff of grand honor. Come on. Don't do this. I'm trying to give you a chance here."

"Honor is a matter of perspective." The man's gaze flicked from one woman to the other. "Is there no chance we can come to some kind of compromise? I can provide compensation for ignoring our efforts. You're not defending a great man. You're defending a money-hungry fool who acquired something he shouldn't have."

"Oh, come on. Do you really think I can agree to that? If all people needed to do to get me to go away was bribe me, I think I'd have a different reputation."

He shook his head. "No, I didn't believe you would agree to such an offer and that's actually a relief. I'd respect you less if you did. But you made a mistake, Dark Princess. You've underestimated us. I'll admit your strategy did deceive us, but we still have our tricks."

One of the wizards snapped his wand up and muttered a hasty spell. A wavering field of translucent blue light formed between her and her opponents.

Alison layered another shield over herself.

Dad's right. You can have the biggest rep in the world but people still fight or run.

Hana sighed and drew her sword. "Because we never, ever encountered a shield before. Seriously? You need to up your game, boys."

"I apologize," he stated. "But as professionals, you have to understand. We have to kill you because it's clear that's the only way we'll be able to kill our target."

"Bring it on," the Drow challenged.

The wizards all lowered their wands and chanted together. She didn't recognize the spell but the ground shook and rattled the windows of the nearby buildings.

She sprouted shadow wings and bounced back. Hana crouched low, her hands tight around her sword, and growled.

A gigantic fist formed from the asphalt erupted behind the wizards and another appeared a second later. They raised until they were each joined by a full body also comprised of asphalt. The wizards hurried behind the growing giants.

"Huh," Alison observed. "I can't say I ever fought something like that before."

CHAPTER TWO

When Alison drew her arm back, streams of light and shadow magic twined together into a growing magical spear. Two more giants grew from the alley at the same time. Each asphalt humanoid towered over them, easily twice her height and more. Despite the mass of the summoned creatures, they left no holes in the road surface. They took loud, ponderous steps forward and their heavy footfalls echoed in the confined area.

She released the spear and it drilled into the shield, then exploded in a shower of sparks. The barrier rippled and vanished.

"It's of no concern," the bearded wizard insisted. "We've already bolstered our numbers."

"The client is almost at the target location," Tahir reported.

Once he arrived, he'd at least be safe for a day, but the team needed to ensure the assassins were dealt with in a more permanent manner. That would likely be settled in the present battle.

"A, do you need help?" Mason asked over the comms.

"You and Drysi continue support for Jerry's team," Alison ordered, her attention locked on the wizards and asphalt giants in front of her. "Hana and I can handle these guys." She looked at the fox. "Take the soft targets and I'll handle the tough ones."

"My baby can cut through anything," the woman insisted and shook her sword.

"I'd rather not test it. It's not like we'll be able to replace it easily. Focus on the soft targets. Uh...the wizards."

"Whatever. It still sounds fun." Hana surged forward. A massive asphalt hand swatted her with surprising speed. She careened into a nearby brick wall with a grunt and hissed as she fell to land in a crouch. The red glow around her skin dimmed slightly. "Those guys are faster than I expected," she muttered.

The wizard smiled. "Don't you see? How can you win against the very environment? We're not like the gutter trash you're used to fighting."

"We win against weird summoned crap all the time," Alison replied. "And I'm vaguely insulted on behalf of the trash I'm allegedly always fighting. I'm merely not prepared to destroy half of Seattle to kill you. Don't get too full of yourself."

"Then that'll make this easy. We operate under no such restrictions. And now, Dark Princess, I'm afraid you have to die." He thrust his free hand out.

The asphalt giants surged forward. She attacked the first and channeled more magic into her shadow blade. The monster brought its fist down and she darted to the side. Her quick swing removed the hand from the arm. A burst of magic elevated her sufficiently to enable her to behead the giant. She was more annoyed than surprised when the headless creature backhanded her with ease.

With a curse of irritation, she tumbled, landed on her feet, and slid a little. "Of course it doesn't actually need the head. That would have made this too easy."

The colossus lumbered forward, flanked by two others. She met its advance and this time, concentrated on a leg. Her blade sliced easily through the limb and the giant pitched forward. Another kicked at her, but she lurched aside and avoided the blow. The wounded monster wasn't eliminated, however. It dragged itself forward with its arm.

What is this? An asphalt zombie?

The wizards chuckled. They kept their wands pointed at the ground and uttered another group chant. More giants grew from the alley. The dense pack of warriors formed a wall that almost blocked any view of their masters.

Hana leapt up and bounded off the wall. One of the huge attackers swung at her and its fist cracked the brick. She landed and darted between the legs of another to close on the wizards behind them. Fireballs exploded around her, but the fox continued her charge, her sword out and ready to taste blood. She had almost reached a man when a giant lashed out with its leg and punted her ten yards away. The impact with the hard surface of the road drew a grunt of pain and she rolled several times before she scrambled to her feet. A little blood leaked from the side of her mouth and her red glow diminished yet again.

Alison rose beyond the reach of the wounded or complete aberrations. *These guys aren't only fast. They hit hard too. We don't have time to play an attrition game with them.*

The summoned monsters were clustered too closely around the wizards for a clear shot, so she needed a new strategy. She released her blade and concentrated her shadow magic into a small point. It was time to test something she'd practiced with Rasila over the last few weeks.

Both princesses believed that having a few new attacks in their arsenal might be helpful soon. Drae had witnessed Alison fight, and the ambitious princess might already have prepared ways to neutralize her rival's standard attacks. Testing a new attack on mindless summoned piles of asphalt was perfect, especially when she needed to avoid collateral damage.

"My guess is this will be endless if we don't eliminate those wizards," she shouted.

"Give me the opening and I'll do what I do best," Hana responded. She backflipped out of reach of a giant's punch with a growl. "Actually, second-best. Being sexy and fierce is what I do best."

They were running out of time. If the wizards summoned more of the enormous warriors, the fight would be forced out of the alley and onto the street. Innocent people might be hurt.

Alison continued to force magic into a small point in front of her. Unlike many of her spells, the concentration of magic grew darker until a dense shadow hung in the air, ringed by wisps of dark purple. A bolt of electricity blasted from between the giants and was joined by fireballs almost immediately. She grimaced as they exploded against her shield. A stinging sensation radiated through her body, but she ignored the attacks and concentrated on feeding her spell.

Hana darted between huge fists and legs and laughed with what might have been abandon. "This is a good work-out. You should summon these in the training room."

When the Drow released her spell, a large purple-black ray streaked out in front of her. It rocketed directly through several of the giants and left gaping holes. A wizard screamed when he became a victim of the attack as well. The creatures all stopped moving.

The fox raced forward and dodged between the killer statues toward the men behind them. She only managed a couple of seconds of unchallenged motion, but it was enough to bring her beside one of her targets. She sank her blade into his chest before she darted away to avoid another blow. The giants had recovered.

Alison shoved her hands forward to launch orbs of light magic toward the wizards. The asphalt monsters moved away from Hana to shield the men. Orbs detonated and hurled debris in every direction as the attacks slowly but steadily chipped away at the giants.

They haven't summoned any new ones. There has to be a limit, and it has to be lower now that there are two less wizards.

"The client is secure," Tahir announced.

"We're coming, A," Mason shouted into his transmitter.

Her husband had made his displeasure clear earlier concerning the plan. That was something that had happened on more than a few occasions whenever he didn't have the chance to be at her side. In the end, however, even if they were husband and wife and Mason a former bodyguard, he always acquiesced to whatever final plan she selected. At work, she was in charge and he would never undermine her authority.

"I can't guarantee we'll leave you anyone," she responded. She continued to pelt the alley with her explosive orbs.

The surviving wizards tried to retaliate with a barrage of coordinated fireballs, which only shoved her back a few yards and didn't pierce her shields.

They're barely attacking, which means they have to put all their effort into controlling the monsters. It's all over but the crying.

Alison flew toward the back of the alley and channeled magic into growing a bigger explosive orb. The enemy hadn't been foolish enough to leave themselves vulnerable in the rear, but there were far fewer giants there compared to the front. Again, the asphalt warriors froze for a few critical seconds. She released her attack and the orb streaked into the back of the formation and exploded. The attack shattered several of them and littered the area with rubble. More importantly, it exposed the surviving wizards.

She directed her flight toward them and hurled a few rapid shadow crescents. One man collapsed with a groan before the remaining massive defenders surged from the front to form a new barrier.

Hana, no longer their focus, vaulted forward and atop a giant. She raced over their heads like she was crossing a mosh pit. Given what Alison had seen at True Portal, Hana's little asphalt giant crowd surfing was almost mundane. At least the monsters had physical bodies.

The Drow spun and elevated at the last moment to

evade a few blows from the creatures. The fox dropped into the center of the formation and immediately began to slice and stab the closely packed wizards. Their wands clattered against the road surface until only the bearded man remained. She held the tip of her blade to his throat, a hungry gleam in her eye.

"Drop the wand," she ordered. "And raise your hands. I'm sure the police, FBI, and PDA would love you to answer a few questions about your stupid little magical assassins' guild. I'm not that angry since you didn't tear my new coat."

The wizard swallowed nervously. His gaze shifted from Alison to Hana before he released his wand and raised his arms slowly.

"They say the Dark Princess is merciful to those who surrender," he stated. "Is that the truth?"

Alison flew toward him. "Yeah, you can say that, but you know what, asshole? The time to give up would have been in the beginning."

The giants remained rigid, more statues than guardians. She flew several passes through the formation to sever legs and arms until only a strange pile filled the alley. It would be stupid to risk the chance of an ambush.

Once she'd resolved that potential threat to her satisfaction, she landed in front of the prisoner and released the magic fueling her wings. She pointed to cracks in the brick walls on either side of the alley and then to a huge hole in the ground. "I can repair that easily enough, so you're lucky. The last thing I wanted to deal with was you destroying a rare item inside that wasn't so easily fixed.

Why can't you assholes ever simply accept that you're outclassed?"

He sighed and his head slumped. "Everyone has a weakness. I thought I could use your concern against you."

Hana grasped his shoulder and shoved him to his knees. "All you did was piss her off." She sheathed her sword but held her claws to his throat. "Make sure you tell everyone in jail how we totally kicked your ass, including me, Hana Sugimoto. Feel free to make up a sexy nickname for me."

He stared at her in bewilderment. "Huh? Sexy nickname?"

Her boss laughed. "I thought you decided to let that happen organically. You haven't complained about it for a while."

"I said he should make up a sexy nickname for me." Her friend gestured to the prisoner. "I didn't tell him what. See, totally organic."

The wizard groaned. "Please, just knock me out."

Hana rolled her eyes. "Assassins are boring."

CHAPTER THREE

Alison weaved through the crowd of Brownstone employees. Her destination was the drinks table set up near the back of the lobby of the Brownstone Building. Although the spacious room could accommodate a good number of people, the growth of the company meant it might not be the best place for events.

I should talk to Ava about adding some kind of banquet hall or something. We have more than enough space on the lot, and I have the money. I might as well spend it on making my employees happier.

Everyone chatted lightheartedly as they sipped their drinks or ate the food provided, mostly delivery pizza and various cheeses and fruits. The office party wasn't a study in expensive elegance, but everyone looked like they were having a good time. It wasn't bad for something thrown together so quickly.

Ava stood at the drinks table and surveyed the crowd with her careful gaze. It was a party, but she looked like she could snatch a hidden weapon and kill an assassin with ease. It wouldn't be a surprise, her boss decided. She'd long since accepted that her assistant had hidden depths and skills.

The woman lifted a pitcher of deep red punch, filled a small cup as Alison approached, and offered the drink to her. "Miss Brownstone, I trust you're having an entertaining time. I apologize for the crudeness of the event."

She shook her head. "That's all my fault. You've told me for a while to have office parties, and I've dragged my feet. You did great considering I dropped all this in your lap with barely any notice, but everyone seems happy, so I'm happy."

"Morale is an important part of any organization that deals consistently in danger," Ava responded. "Especially when it's more than a small group of people." She frowned slightly as she looked at a banner over the doorway. "I know you let Miss Sugimoto decide the name for this particular event, but I do think that 'Asskickers' Ball' lacks a certain...quality that I associate with Brownstone Security."

"She was so happy about it. I didn't want to disappoint her." She chuckled. "But duly noted. Maybe next time, we'll put it to a vote."

"I think that's for the best. People enjoy feeling like they're stakeholders, even in events of minor importance." The woman pursed her lips.

The laughing and talking crowd choked the lobby and spilled into the connecting hallway. Besides the core magicals of Mason, Hana, Drysi, Tahir, and Sonya, Jerry and his team provided the greatest number of employees. But the business couldn't function only with field teams and their direct support staff. Brownstone Security thrived because of the contributions of a variety of personnel, everyone from the administrative assistants like Sienna and the company chef who chatted to one of the security guards close to the front. They had made a point to order food to ensure that everyone, including the chef, could have a good time.

I ask so much from them, and this building has been targeted before. I need to do more. It's one thing to say I care, but I need to show them I care. This is a small way to do that, but at least it's something.

Alison took a sip of her punch. "Thanks for handling all the logistics as usual, Ava. I don't know how I would have grown this business without all your help. It'd probably merely be Hana and I running around like bad PIs in an old detective movie or something." She laughed when she recalled their first few jobs together. These days, they had Tahir and Sonya to do most of their research. It meant they didn't have to rely on sneaking into strange motels and using Hana's charm and con-woman skills to pull information out of unsuspecting people.

It'd been a different company in the beginning. She missed it at times but was proud of what Brownstone Security had grown into as well.

This is why I need to be careful with the Drow crap. If Drae and the Guardians are willing to pull stunts like they did, there is no guarantee they won't eventually come here. Should I simply send everyone on vacation until it's over? I don't know. It could be a matter of days before it's resolved, or it could be months.

Every time I think it'll happen, something delays the final confrontation.

She sighed.

"Is there a problem, Miss Brownstone?" Ava asked.

"No, I'm merely overthinking."

"There's no such thing as overthinking. There is only being prepared or unprepared, and you are generally prepared." Her assistant smiled. "It's been my pleasure to see you grow as a security contractor and a magical." She leaned closer and lowered her voice. "I want to admit something I never did before, Miss Brownstone. I suppose it's long overdue."

"What's that? Do you want a raise?" She grinned.

"No, I'm more than satisfied with my compensation, and it's not as if I need it," Ava replied. There were still so many details of the woman's life Alison didn't know. From what she had gathered, she used to work for British intelligence and at least played some role or had contact with the UK's equivalent of the CIA's Non-Oriceran Alien Task Force before she did something that forced her to leave her home country. Given how loyally she had served at Brownstone Security, she assumed she had been kicked out for doing the right thing but annoying some of her superiors.

Now, she merely nodded and waited for the rest of the explanation.

"Part of the reason I took this job was to keep an eye on you," the woman continued. "Not officially. I'm strictly a private operative at this point, but I've been aware of your father since the incident in LA."

Alison frowned. "He saved—"

Ava cut her off with a raised eyebrow. "I know. He's powerful and dangerous in his own way. Your adoptive mother is an intelligent and dangerous woman with...a colorful background. She's settled into a fine life as an academic but given what she was doing and her involvement in unusual affairs, one could be forgiven for being suspicious. You had a good reputation as a tough but honest bounty hunter, but that's not the same thing as being trustworthy, especially after you spent time on Oriceran with the Drow. As recent experiences have demonstrated, not all your people can be trusted."

"That can be said for humans as well."

"Of course, but the average human isn't as powerful as the average Drow."

She took a sip of her punch and realized she couldn't hear anything else in the room. There hadn't been any magic, so her assistant must be using a silence cube—another leftover from her hidden past, most likely.

"Okay, fair enough," she replied with no accusation or anger in her voice. Ava had never been so direct about her motivations before. A magically encrypted cipher was clear compared to the English woman, but that changed nothing. Whatever her reasons for joining, she was integral to the success of Brownstone Security and she couldn't imagine the company without her. "What about now? Since I'm not dead, I assume you determined that you can trust me. I don't care if you're not a magical. I know you could assassinate me if you set your mind to it."

"Let us hope it never comes to that." The woman smiled slightly. "And I doubt it will. You have exceeded my wildest expectations and hopes. Not to demean your father, but you're a vast improvement upon him in that you have power, temperament, and a desire to use your power to help others, whereas he simply wants to be left alone and attracts excess trouble due to his nature. I'm glad I interviewed for the job. I think I would have regretted not being involved with you." Her breath caught and uncertainty flickered across her face. "And I'll also admit I needed it as much as you did. It's good to belong to a place that provides meaning." The ambient chatter returned. "But you should circulate, Miss Brownstone. There are many people who would like facetime with their boss."

"Thanks again for everything."

"My pleasure." The woman inclined her head.

Alison topped her punch off before she wandered away from the table. Drysi leaned against a wall a few yards away and munched on a plate of crackers and cheddar slices. She moved toward her.

"You need more booze at this party," the Welsh witch insisted. She gestured toward her cup. "You could have at least spiked that. Whoever heard of a party without alcohol? I thought about using magic but the damned stuff never comes out right when I do. It's not tidy at all."

She laughed. "Ava and I discussed that. We probably will have some next time." She inclined her head toward Sonya across the room. The girl waved her arms and smiled brightly as she chatted with Sienna and Tahir. A follow-up pantomime suggested they were discussing drone battle racing. "It's nice to have a party where she can fully participate. I know some of us like to party harder than others. We'll have more events like this going forward, not only the seasonal ones. We can divide them by type."

"But I want fucking alcohol." Drysi scoffed. "I drank more whisky than water by the time I was her age."

Her boss chuckled. "I didn't. I can only imagine what Headmistress Berens would have done to us if we ran around getting drunk at the School of Necessary Magic."

"There's your problem. You went to that prissy fucking magic school." The witch tossed another cheddar slice in her mouth. "There were advantages to growing up the way I did. It taught me so much about the world."

Alison looked around and furrowed her brow. Her gaze drifted from person to person, but there was one notice-able absence. "Have you seen Hana? She mentioned having to get something ready but that was a while ago." She glanced at Tahir again, but his girlfriend was nowhere to be seen and the nine-tailed fox was not the kind of woman who blended in with a crowd.

Drysi shook her head but a grin built. "Maybe she went to get booze. Whatever else you can say about her, she knows how to party."

The infomancer yanked his phone from his pocket and stared at it. His eyes narrowed. He whispered something to Sonya before he pushed through the crowd toward the front of the room. A moment later, Hana sprinted to the front door from the outside and threw it open.

"I'm here!" she sang at the top of her lungs.

Everyone stopped and stared at her.

She sauntered inside and closed the door before she waved and opened her red overcoat to reveal a short, crimson latex mini-dress she hadn't worn thirty minutes before. "Hi, everyone. Now that we're all gathered, I have an announcement." She threw her arms around Tahir. "Well, he has an announcement. We both do? He'll do the talking first." She laughed.

Murmurs rippled through the crowd.

He sighed, raised a hand to his face, and cleared his throat. "I don't see a point in dragging this out since the relevant parties have already had the most important discussion, so I'll simply come out and say it. Yesterday, I asked Hana to marry me. To absolutely no one's surprise, she readily agreed to the proposal."

Everyone fell silent. A few seconds later, the room erupted in cheers and claps. His face twitched but the fox's smile grew larger. Tahir took a deep breath and exhaled slowly, looking embarrassed at all the attention.

Mason, who had been talking to Jerry in the center of the room, stepped forward. He waited for the claps and cheers to die down. "You're right. I can't say it's a big surprise, but congratulations, you two." He grinned. "I'll put in a good word for married life." He winked at Alison.

The infomancer nodded at him. "Hana has made it clear that she desires more than what we currently share, and it's only logical to take the next step since I'm doubtful I'll ever do better than her. She certainly is superior to all previous women I've dated."

Hana giggled. "I do rock."

Alison chuckled. It was blunt but honest and even kind of romantic—and pure Tahir. He might not be a sweet-talker like Mason, but he did all right in his own way. He'd also changed.

When she had first met him, he was an arrogant bastard

more interested in toying with her and proving his superiority. The idea of him caring enough about anyone to want to either help or spend the rest of his life with them would have seemed absurd. Now, he had an apprentice and a fiancée.

Is that why she asked about Izzie? I'm surprised she didn't tell me before, but I'm glad for them. I'm also kind of scared of what she'll come up with.

Hana tightened her arm around Tahir. "And you're damned straight. I'm the total package." She ruffled his hair. After a final squeeze, she released him. "And because of certain people who aren't patient, I need to make it clear this won't be a boring Vegas quickie where you don't find out until after it's over and done with."

The crowd chuckled. Most people glanced at Alison and Mason and she smiled sheepishly and shrugged. She stood by her decision, but she knew more than a few people who would have loved to have been at her wedding.

"It'll be gorgeous, over-the-top, and ridiculous," the woman declared, threw her arms up, and confirmed her boss' worst fears. "Exactly like me. The wedding won't be for at least a year. That kind of awesomeness needs to be planned carefully. By the way, if anyone knows where I can rent a Zeppelin, let me know."

Everyone laughed, but Alison suspected she wasn't joking.

Sienna sighed. "He didn't ask you right now, did he?" She eyed the infomancer with suspicion.

He snorted. "Certainly not," he insisted. "What, you think I proposed to her over the phone?"

"Maybe?" The woman shrugged. "It kind of seems like

something you'd do, and she didn't tell any of us this was coming."

Tahir frowned.

Hana's first response was another loud giggle. "Secrets can be fun. But I wanted to let you know you're all invited. Keep an eye out for your save-the-date. You won't want to miss the Sugimoto-Arain wedding."

The crowd cheered and clapped again.

Alison smiled warmly at her friend. The announcement crystallized something that had lingered in the back of her mind since the start of the party. Brownstone Security wasn't merely a business she'd grown. The people in the room were more than only employees. They were family. Every success, every child, and every marriage grew that family.

I'm finally starting to understand what Dad put together with the Brownstone Agency.

After a few minutes of working the crowd with excited declarations about how glorious her wedding would be, Hana grabbed Alison by the arm and tugged her through the hallway and around the corner. They escaped the crowd and the party din reduced to a quiet, distant murmur. Tahir had been surrounded by everyone who wanted to give their congratulations and praise him as if they were worried he might call it off when he got annoyed later.

The fox clapped and bounced on the balls of her feet.

"It's so exciting. I admit, I pressed him a little, but he was heading that way anyway." Her eyes glistened.

"What's wrong?" she asked. "Are you okay?"

The woman wiped her tears away with her wrist. "They are happy tears, not sad tears, and it's not only about Tahir —even though that's totally awesome. Since I have piles of money from working here, I seriously intend to have the ultimate wedding. It'll be the kind of occasion they write epic legends about later." She threw her arms around her friend and yanked her into a tight hug. "It's happening."

"I...can't...breathe," she wheezed.

Hana chuckled and released her. "Oh, sorry about that. I owe this all to you, so it's hard to keep it all in."

Alison took a few breaths. "Me? I didn't say anything to Tahir about getting married and despite what you said, I don't think my marriage had that much of an effect. There are many people in relationships in the company who aren't getting married."

The fox sniffled and wiped another tear away. "No, I'm not talking about that." She flung her hand toward a wall. "That."

"The wall?" She stared at it and wondered what she was supposed to see.

"This place. This job. When we met, I saw you as nothing but a mark. I'd lived a self-absorbed life conning people, and I planned to use you to get out of trouble." She sighed. "Once you realized what I was doing, you could have killed me. We both know many people would have, given what I tried to do, but not only did you not kill me, you helped me. You pulled me out of all that garbage."

"I had my own reasons for that," she insisted. "Don't put me on too high a pedestal."

Hana rolled her eyes. "Please. Don't even try to give me the ruthless vengeance line. You could have eliminated that guy without helping me. Even if you didn't kill me, you could also have easily had me arrested. You might be the Dark Princess now but back then, you were still merely Alison Brownstone. You gave me everything. A job, a place to belong, and friendship." She sucked in a shuddering breath. "I wouldn't have met the love of my life if it wasn't for you. Meeting you was the best thing in my life. If I were into chicks, I would have totally married you."

Alison laughed. Her cheeks heated and she looked away. "All I did was give you a chance. You're the one who took it. Some of the people I offer chances to throw them away."

"There are so many people in this company and this city whom you've saved." Hana pointed to the ceiling. "The world. You've made a big difference in countless lives, and you could have chosen to do nothing or you could have chosen to be an evil Dark Princess. You know, like Drae."

Her stomach tightened but she held her smile. She didn't want to disrupt her friend's emotional high by complaining about Drow politics.

"I would never misuse my power," she replied, "and all I've done is what other people did for me, including my parents. I learned from them. I was scared, and Mom and Dad didn't have to care about me. I wasn't anything to them, merely a kid whose biological father was a piece of shit and whose mom was a strange Drow princess who died and forced a horrible responsibility on someone else."

She blinked the tears in her eyes away. All the emotion was contagious. "I spent most of my early life not sure what I would do with my life, but when I came into my magic, I knew exactly what I wanted to do with it because of the good examples that had been set for me."

Hana patted her on the shoulder. "That's what I'm getting at, Alison. You're not only our cool boss. You're not only our Dark Princess we live to serve. You set an example we all want to live up to. Drysi was an assassin for dark wizards and you turned her into a good person. Well...an okay person." She let out a contented sigh. "I have one more favor I need from you."

"Sure. What did you need?"

The woman grinned. "Don't worry. It won't involve too much effort because I'll do all the work when it comes to my wedding."

She backed away. "Now, I'm worried. What are you talking about?"

"I want you to be my maid of honor."

Alison uttered a single sharp laugh. "Oh. That's it? Sure. I'd love to, Hana." She scratched her cheek. "I do have one idea, though. It's only a suggestion."

The fox folded her arms and defiance settled on her face. Her puffy eyes and reddened cheeks weakened the look. "I have very particular plans for the wedding. Tahir will stay out of the way of this bridezilla fox, but I'm willing to listen."

"I'm not talking about that kind of thing. I simply wondered if we can improve city security at the same time."

"How?"

She smiled. "By pulling a Brownstone. We do what Dad did. We force all the big underworld guys to appear to put them on notice."

Hana laughed. "As long as they bring nice gifts, I don't care. If you're a Mafia don, you should be able to do better than a toaster as a gift."

CHAPTER FOUR

Drae stood in the center of a large clearing. Tall, dark trees surrounded her on all sides and their thick limbs obscured most of the light of the stars and Oriceran's two moons. A few creatures stirred, fluttered through the leafy branches, or scuttled through the underbrush, but none approached her. Red eyes appeared in the darkness, followed by a soft growl.

She turned toward the beast and smiled.

The creature whimpered and pushed deeper into the vegetation, no longer the vicious hunter. It remained alive longer if it recognized the alpha predator.

Soon. It'll happen soon. I've been so patient, but it will all pay off.

Alison Brownstone's power necessitated careful planning. Drae was disappointed that the Princess of the Shadow Forged had managed to escape the event that caused Miar's demise unscathed but she wasn't completely surprised, which is why she'd taken the appropriate precautions. The half-human's concern over innocent deaths provided a measure of control, but she had proven that when pushed too far, she could deliver vicious retribution equal to Queen Laena's past efforts.

Perhaps fate is testing the Drow. Laena failed against James Brownstone, but I will not fail against his daughter. I will rise to the occasion.

None of these challenges meant that victory wasn't close. Both Miar and Novati were dead. The Guardians were in disarray. Several members had already been executed, and many of the Drow saw them as weak schemers too afraid to face the princesses directly. Each day, more challenged their authority and pledged loyalty to one of the remaining princesses. Once Alison and Rasila were killed, it would be a simple matter to exterminate the Guardians and restore a proper monarchy. A new queen would lead them into the future. The mistakes of the past would be washed away by blood.

Branches crunched nearby and the howl of the wind almost covered the sound.

"I expected you earlier," she declared without turning toward the source of the noise. Novati and Laena had punished failure severely, but she understood that a light touch of implied terror could be so much more effective. She jerked her arm up. A dark blast of magic split a tree in the distance in half.

Her visitor stepped out of the shadows. A tall Drow warrior, Marat had served Novati originally, although Drae had turned him to her cause to great effect. Without his previous aid, her last plan might not have succeeded.

"These are dangerous times, my princess," he explained with a bow. "I need to be careful to not be seen. If I lose my position among the remnants of Princess Novati's forces, I will not be able to be of further service to your great cause. I wish to do my best to continue to aid you with your coming victories."

She craned her neck upward and locked her gaze on a particularly bright star, so beautiful and distant. "That's reasonable, but the question remains whether you truly believe that or if you're nothing more than an opportunist. Some might see me that way, but everything I have done has been to strengthen and unify my people."

"I'm not an opportunist," he snapped and his face contorted in anger. "I aided your scheme against the Guardians and Princess Novati, despite my earlier pledges. I did that because I believed in what you told me about the future of the Drow."

Still, she didn't face him and continued to stare at the star. "That was the betrayal of pretenders and one arrogant woman. It's trivial for anyone with true strength of will. My question is, are you prepared to do what is necessary when others of less ambition will be hurt? Can you hurt people who aren't truly your enemies?"

Marat squared his shoulders and raised his chin. "I am, and I will. I would never have helped you to begin with, otherwise. We've been adrift too long, and I know your plan will help right that for our people. I understand that. If I didn't believe it, I would have stayed at Novati's side."

"Good. I'm happy to hear that." Drae lowered her head slowly. "We'll have to move quickly. If we wait too long, Alison and Rasila will have too much time to consolidate the additional forces they've inherited. Wounding the Guardians was sufficient to control them, but the princesses will not remain cowed. Soon, they will come to the conclusion that the only solution to the problem is the one I've already reached—the total elimination of all competitors."

"I'll do whatever you need of me, Princess Drae, no matter what the cost or risk."

Finally, she turned to face the man. "I spoke too politely earlier. My plan does not involve simply hurting the innocent. It will cost many Drow lives. Whether I do this out of antipathy toward those lives or not doesn't negate that truth. Some might not understand what we have to do. I need to be sure that you do."

His determined expression didn't change. "This is a war, Princess."

"Yes, it is. What of it?"

"In war, there are always innocent casualties."

A ripple of magic caught her attention. It was subtle and almost imperceptible and shadows shifted behind her companion in a way only a Drow could appreciate.

Ah. They've already made their move.

Drae flung her hand up. A tenebrous dagger tinged with purple materialized and streaked toward Marat.

His eyes widened. "Princess Drae, you have—"

The weapon passed over his shoulder and stopped in midair. A woman cried out but there was no one else in the clearing.

The princess extended a shadow blade and strode forward. Marat turned slowly. The dagger hovered in what seemed to be empty space, but blood dripped from the blade. The air shimmered and a Drow woman appeared. The weapon was embedded in her chest.

She fell to her knees, hissed in pain, and yanked the weapon out. Tendrils of shadow extended over her wound and knitted it closed.

"I applaud your audacity even as I question your intelligence." Drae smiled and pointed her shadow blade at the woman's neck. "Did you really think I wouldn't be able to discern you?"

The spy glared at her. "I have my orders from Princess Rasila. Now, I understand what you've done."

"Princess Rasila will be dead soon," she declared. "And you won't tell her anything before that."

The wind picked up and scuttered a few branches and leaves through the clearing. Marat conjured a shadow blade and looked around, his brow wrinkled with worry.

"Princess Rasila didn't fall for your tricks," the woman shouted. "Princess Alison might be a warrior like Novati and Miar, but Princess Rasila is clever. She sees right through you."

Drae didn't move her blade. "I won't insult you by pretending I had nothing to do with what happened, but I want you to consider the implications of what you've said. All has proceeded according to my plans and my efforts. Two princesses are already dead, and they lack clear heirs. Alison and Rasila have been led around by my efforts, dancing like puppets for me. Why continue to serve a woman who will be dead? Spare me bold declarations of Rasila's honor. She would kill me if she had the chance and only didn't because she doesn't wish to anger Alison."

"You've proven yourself no better than Laena." The spy sneered. "I heard you speaking to that traitor. Do you think you'll lead us to something great? You'll lead us to self-destruction."

Marat continued his patrol, although the concern on his face eased somewhat.

The princess chuckled. "I'm no better than Laena? Perhaps that's true, but one can't deny that when she was queen, the Drow were feared. Now, we're considered unimportant. The Light Elves and their allies only watch us because they know a queen will rise soon."

"Yes, a queen who isn't you," the woman shouted.

She clucked her tongue. "You were brave to come here and I value that, so I don't wish to throw your life away unnecessarily. I would also prefer to offer you another perspective. Even if Rasila somehow survives all this, she has no grander plan than to become the slave of that half-breed. Is that what you want for our people—to be ruled by someone more human than Drow?"

"I support Princess Rasila," the spy insisted. "And if she supports Princess Alison for queen, then I support Princess Alison for queen."

"Then you're offering your life."

Calmly, she raised her head to expose her neck. "I'm prepared to die for my princess and my queen. When this is all over, Drae, you will be dead and your schemes nothing but bitter ashes in your mouth. Your name will be reviled for tricks and lack of honor."

Drae scoffed. "So be it. You've made your choice." She decapitated the woman in one stroke. "Then die for her."

Marat eyed the corpse with a faint sneer. "You did the right thing, my princess."

"I know." Her blade vanished and she turned toward

him. "But the fact that Rasila got a spy this close to me only confirms that we must move faster. I have a special task for you, Marat."

He bowed his head. "I live to serve, my princess." He smiled. "No. I live to serve, my queen."

CHAPTER FIVE

Alison settled into a chair in front of Agent Latherby. She'd been content to talk wedding plans with Hana the day after the party, but the PDA agent had called her out of the blue and requested a meeting. He wasn't the social kind, which meant he needed her for a dangerous job and one potentially off the books.

This is all part of what Hana talked about. If I want to save the world, I occasionally need to do a little work on my day off.

She had hoped for a good week or so off following the last operation and the party, especially with the coming holiday. Halloween had grown more fraught in recent years. As the gates continued to open, the increased magic made the veil thinner during the special day. In the past, someone might only have to worry about that kind of thing near a kemana, but it wasn't so easy to do that anymore. The types of spirits one might run into on Halloween weren't friendly little white ghosts who looked like sheets.

"Okay, you called and I'm here." She shrugged. "And I

came alone like you asked. I hope this doesn't end with you trying to kill me." She sensed a higher level of magic in the office than normal.

A twitch of his mouth suggested he was in danger of evidencing a smile, but he managed to maintain his staid façade. "No, Miss Brownstone. If, for some reason, I thought you had become a danger, I don't think I would be so foolish as to ever attempt to apprehend you in a location that I didn't expect would be destroyed in the process. You've long since proven that you can defend yourself with or without your associates and husband."

She chuckled. "Jeez, Latherby, it was only a joke." She hoped so because she didn't want to have to attack someone she respected. He'd helped her even when he didn't need to in the past.

His mouth twitched again and something approaching fear flashed in his eyes. She rarely saw him like this and it unsettled her. After a moment, he regained his composure.

"I have a special job for you," he explained. "Because of the narrow time window, I need someone trustworthy, strong in magic, and who can travel quickly. I want to be upfront about what this will involve. Please note I'm taking extra measures to keep this conversation private."

Alison frowned. "That explains the magic I sense. Are we talking about more infiltration of the PDA? Dark wizards? Maybe Seventh Order holdouts?"

He shook his head. "Nothing so straightforward. Let us simply say it would be more accurate to describe this as a request rather than a job. Many of my superiors think this matter should be left well enough alone. In this case, I won't even be able to pay you, but I'm more than willing to owe you a favor. I want to be honest with you, Miss Brownstone. I'm asking for your help less as a member of the PDA than as a private citizen. Consider this a personal favor."

"Okay," she responded warily. "Let me get one question out of the way before I ask for the kind of details that will end with CIA assassins on my ass. Does this favor involve danger to innocent people?"

"Not in the conventional sense. That's why the government can afford to look the other way on this matter."

She nodded. "I see. I'm not saying no, but you'll need to sell me on this. I wanted to take it easy over the next couple of weeks, if only because I need to be ready to move if Drae tries something."

"I understand." The agent folded his hands in front of him, all hint of vulnerability gone from his face. "Have you ever heard of the Philadelphia Experiment?"

"A little. A Navy destroyer ran experiments during World War II. Officially, it was only anti radar focused and people blew it out of proportion, but there have since been rumors that the experiment was something more—something supernatural. It used to be that people said it was some kind of high-tech invisibility experiment, but ever since the truth of magic came out, people have moved on to say it was a magical portaling attempt. The claim is that since the experiment violated all kinds of rules about concealing magic, everyone involved tried to keep it secret and they botched it somehow at the time." She shrugged and made no effort to hide the incredulity on her face. "I find it hard to believe that anyone portaled big Navy boats around before the gates began to open."

Agent Latherby stared at her in silence for an uncomfortably long time. "Be that as it may, it's partially true. It wasn't a magical portaling experiment. It was a direct teleportation experiment conducted by a small group of American wizards who understood that it might get them in trouble but who did have some support from their superiors. They used certain artifacts to hide what they were doing and provide the necessary magical energy. My predecessors in the government made sure to cover it up. The actual experiment didn't occur in Philadelphia but in the ocean near Hawaii. The best lies always have an element of truth."

"Don't I know it."

"Before the PDF, there was another group, known as Project X and they always denied any official government involvement in anything like that, but they definitely knew. Once Project X became the PDF, it continued to deny involvement, even when the truth about magic came out." He sighed. "There were many concerns during the war. Both sides broke numerous treaties and rules concerning magic. I don't know all the details, but I know some of the motivations for the experiment were attempts to counter similar German and Japanese experiments. Groups like the Griffins tried to keep things in check, as did the Fixer at the time, but nations focused on war aren't so easily controlled."

Alison absorbed all the information. It was far less shocking than many of the other things covered up about magic prior to the gates reopening. In the end, it was merely government CYA with a magical twist.

"The true ship involved in the experiment has been

effectively erased from history," the agent explained. "The USS *Constantinople*. The experiment itself was performed on Halloween in 1943. It was easy to scrub its official existence since the ship vanished as a result of the experiment itself."

"That's all interesting." Her stomach tightened. "But where do I come in? I'm powerful and can portal, but I have my limits. I can't time travel."

"Of course not." He swallowed and his eyes remained fixed on her as if he were evaluating whether she would agree or not. "As I noted, the *Constantinople* was lost during the experiment. The government manipulated the records to make it look like the various sailors on board had died in different places to avoid any evidence of what they were doing. The only hint that the ship itself ever existed is irregularities in the Naval vessel records. Even though they never intended to mention magic in official records at the time, the ship was still already somewhat cloaked under a veil of secrecy because it was a testbed ship."

Veil. Alison froze at the word and decided she needed to establish something before they continued the conversation. "It disappeared on Halloween. I don't care how powerful you think I am, Latherby, I can't go into the World in Between and get back. I won't. I've heard enough about how terrible that can be."

He scoffed. "Of course, and I don't expect that. Fortunately, that's not where the *Constantinople* ended up—not all the way, at least."

"Not all the way? You honestly don't make this sound any better."

"The veil between worlds thins on Halloween. The

Constantinople isn't completely in the World in Between because people have seen it here on Halloween—not a mere shadow but the whole ship. My theory is that it's almost stuck halfway between our world and there. It has appeared several times since the original 1943 experiment. Not every year but enough times for additional legends to grow around it. It's not always in the same location, either, but it's always in a sea or ocean."

She frowned. "If the government scrubbed all this information before you were born, how do you even know about it? And if I agree to this insane request to mess with a century-old ship that is stuck between worlds or whatever, how am I supposed to find it if it's not always in the same place?"

Agent Latherby opened a desk drawer, retrieved a small palm-sized silver music box, and set in front of him. Faint magic radiated off the object.

"What's that?" she asked.

"A gift," he related. "More specifically, it was a gift from one of the officers on the *Constantinople* to his wife."

No obvious runes or magical symbols decorated it. Maybe it was exactly what it appeared.

"A magic music box? The 1940s version of a portable music player?"

He shook his head. "Think of it as more of a transmitter and link. The officer on the *Constantinople* was a wizard from a distinguished family of wizards. His wife also came from a long line of magicals but she lacked any active magical talent. When he was deployed to Hawaii, she had to remain in Ohio, but she knew he was involved in magical experiments. She also knew he was uncomfortable with them and had tried to talk the others out of them. Not only that, she was pregnant at the time."

The man frowned and shook his head. "She knew something had gone wrong because her husband was able to send one last message—'Don't ask them about it and forgive me. The only thing I can do is save you and our baby.'" He took a deep breath and stared into the distance, lost in his own thoughts for a moment. "The government, of course, fed her a line about him dying in a traffic accident in San Diego. She understood that whatever happened likely involved magic and she didn't question it. Her decision was the only possible one under the circumstances. She didn't want to mysteriously disappear or have her memories wiped."

Alison leaned forward. It was hard to tear her attention from the music box. There was an aura about the artifact that demanded she focus on it. "But you said this was personal. I already have an inkling about why that is, but let's get it out there so we're both on the same page."

"That wizard, Ensign Abner Latherby, was my great-grandfather," the agent admitted. "And I believe he and the other sailors are still trapped on the *Constantinople.* Those men don't deserve to be stuck in a twisted magical purgatory halfway between realities. My great-grandfather was already upset about the experiment, and the average man on the ship didn't know what they'd signed up for. It's cruel that they've been left there."

"I don't mean to be a bitch, but how do you know they're still alive?"

"Once I became aware of my family legacy, I spent years studying the sightings. Witnesses have mentioned forms that resemble sailors, and at least one person described someone moving on the ship. All the stories indicate that clear perception is difficult because of a kind of magical haze or dome—these vary depending on the story—but there are clearly still people there."

She swallowed a little uncomfortably and couldn't believe she was seriously considering hunting what was effectively a ghost ship—one the government didn't want anyone to know about. There was also a more immediate practical consideration.

After a moment, she sighed. "Let's say I agree to help you. You've already told me it's not always in the same location, and it doesn't always appear every year. So what am I supposed to do? Fly around the world on Halloween like Jack Skellington?"

"Who?" Agent Latherby waved a hand quickly. "Never mind. I know it'll appear because the music box is still linked to my great-grandfather. My family's lore says the enchantment will end when he dies. It always plays a tune two weeks before an appearance of the *Constantinople*. It hasn't played for ten years but this year, it did. I didn't have the music box ten years ago—another relative did, one too afraid to help him and the sailors. But now we have a chance to make things right."

He pointed at her. "Those men deserve to be at rest. You're uniquely qualified for this, Miss Brownstone, with your portaling and general magical strength. You can use the music box as a tracking focus and reach the ship in the brief period when it manifests between sunset on Halloween and sunrise." He lowered his hand. "Technically, I'm asking you to go against the expressed goals of the

PDA and the government in this. I inquired myself shortly after inheriting the music box and presented my interest as resolving the truth of the rumors of the ghost destroyer. It was made clear to me in no uncertain terms that I should keep my nose out of it."

"I doubt the government will harass me in a serious way for solving a mystery if I keep your name out of it. They've let this fester for so long, they're probably more embarrassed than anything else. They'll simply sweep it under the rug again, but we can still save those men." She rubbed the back of her neck. "I have to think about it. If I do it, I won't be able to do it alone. I'll need to include some of my people, and I won't order them into a dangerous mission for no pay that might put them on a watch list."

The agent stood and extended his hand. "Thank you for even considering it. I know you have your own issues given the Drow situation."

Her laugh was a little bitter. "Maybe finding a ghost ship will be a nice way to get my mind off Drae. At least there won't be any Drow assassins on the *Constantinople*."

CHAPTER SIX

"So, that's the quick version," Alison finished. "I haven't agreed to anything yet, but I'm personally thinking about taking it on. Latherby's request is different than our typical job, but I don't think it's any less important. While I know you all joined the company for different reasons, I ultimately wanted to start this company to help people."

The team had convened in the conference room on the morning following her meeting with Agent Latherby. She had wanted time to think things over, but the only thing she knew for certain was that Sonya wouldn't be involved, so she didn't insist that she come to the meeting. Ava might not actually deploy on the mission, but it was rare for any company-related discussion to not have the woman present. She wasn't merely her right hand. Her assistant was almost her brain.

"You should have simply started a damned superhero firm," Drysi muttered.

Hana smirked. "You know you'd love it. Everyone loves villains who become heroes."

The Welsh witch frowned. "I wasn't a fucking villain, Hana. I was an assassin."

"I was a villain." The fox sighed. "I merely didn't have an awesome supervillain name. Lady Night Fox or something like that. Sexy Fox would be too obvious. Oh, Charmafox. It's a combination of charming and fox, get it?"

Tahir cracked a smile. Mason chuckled and shook his head.

Hana pointed at Drysi. "You could be Rainbow Knife Woman or even the Rainbow Knife. It works as a villain name or a hero name. Alison's already Dark Prin—"

Alison cleared her throat loudly. "Can we please stay on task? Let's talk about the *Constantinople* and the job."

"That's right. Hunting a ghost ship." The fox rubbed her hands together. "That is about the coolest thing we will have ever done, I think." Her brow crinkled. "There was that kind of ghost thing in the kemana ruins, but that was more creepy than cool. I hope this is more cool than creepy."

I think she has the wrong attitude about this but I'd rather not discourage anyone from coming along. I might need all the help I can get.

"We might end up ghosts ourselves," Drysi grumbled. "I'm not fond of the idea of trying to make up for a twisted mistake that's kept a ship appearing and reappearing throughout history, even before the gates started reopening. That suggests there was an incredible amount of magic involved, and we've all seen what that can mean."

"It's a good point." Alison looked at Hana. "This isn't a game. It's a rescue mission."

The woman rolled her eyes. "Nothing says it can't be a fun rescue mission, though."

"But keep the reality in mind. I wouldn't bother with this if I didn't think there was some possibility that we could save lives. From what Agent Latherby told me, it's not as if the *Constantinople* is dangerous. I merely hope some sailors are still alive. Despite the horrible mistake that happened with the spell, there were wizards on that ship and they might have had a way to protect people."

Mason raised an eyebrow. "And what if Latherby's wrong and all the men are already dead? We don't know what we might step into with this. You don't know for certain it's not dangerous, A. You've simply made assumptions."

"I still think it's worth taking the chance."

"He's right," Drysi concurred. "Just because the ship's there doesn't mean anyone survived. It's been over a hundred years, Alison. Think about that. Even with a few magicals on board, cut off from Earth and Oriceran, there's only so much they can do. Do you plan to bring all those bodies back? From what you've said, everyone else already believed those men died, so it's not like the families have spent decades wondering what happened to them."

"No, I don't plan to bring any bodies back," she replied. "But if everyone's dead, Latherby's family will at least have some closure. Besides, we don't know what happened. They could all be in some kind of magical suspended animation or in a spirit form and need to be laid to rest."

The witch scoffed. "I thought it was a rescue mission. Now, we're putting their ghosts to rest?"

"That doesn't sound fun," Hana complained.

"I don't know." She sighed. "Neither do you, but I don't like the idea of ignoring them if we could possibly help them. That ship constantly comes back. It has to mean something."

Drysi shook her head slightly. "It might simply mean a dead ship is doomed to disappear and reappear until the universe ends."

"Let's hope not." Alison turned to Tahir. "Did you find anything out? Sorry for the short notice. I wanted to sleep on it and make my decision before I asked any of you but I probably should have asked you last night. I trust Latherby, but I'd prefer it if I had confirmation that some of what he told me was true."

The infomancer scoffed. "Don't underestimate me, Alison. It was a trivial task, even with only a couple of hours of lead time." His gaze dropped to his phone. "I've found nothing that would directly contradict what Agent Latherby told you. I've been able to find multiple sightings of a phantom destroyer throughout the world, all of them occurring after 1943. I will note that despite the length of time since the last sighting, the overall number of sightings has increased since the gates began to open. They had actually become increasingly more common before the hiatus. There are various theories for why the ship vanished thereafter and many people seemed to prefer the idea that the sailors had finally been able to achieve rest." He looked annoyed. "But I didn't find anything to suggest that anyone had any great insight into the true nature of the ship."

She leaned forward and rested her elbows on the table. "Huh. I wonder. If it appeared more often, that makes it sound like they might have been closer to escaping but something changed. It makes me a little more hopeful that we'll still find someone on it."

Tahir shrugged. "Without knowing more about what happened there, I don't think we can speculate with any real accuracy. The only concrete thing we have to go on is that music box, and if Agent Latherby's wrong, either nothing will happen on Halloween or we'll have no way to track it. Even I can't monitor the entire world, Alison."

"That's fine. If nothing happens or we can't find the ship, this will simply have been a waste of time and not a risk at all. I'd rather make an attempt and fail than not try at all. I'm more than happy to go to Latherby and tell him nothing happened. By now, he knows I won't bullshit him."

Mason sighed. "A, this whole ship could be stuck in the World in Between. We might not be able to do anything about it if it's there. It might have appeared in areas of high magical concentration even before the gates started opening."

The infomancer shook his head. "I actually attempted to cross-reference known sightings with known areas of high magical concentration before and after the opening, and I couldn't find any pattern to support that hypothesis. I'm not saying you're wrong, Mason, but we'd need more evidence."

"I understand that we might not succeed, but I at least want to try. If the ship was stuck permanently in the World in Between or even somewhere else, there'd be nothing we could do about it. But if the *Constantinople* appears on Earth, we at least have an opportunity to do something. It's not simply a ghost ship. It's a real ship that's appeared for hours at a time." Alison gestured around the table. "If we have enough raw magical power in this room to fight an alien army and entire sinister magical societies, we have enough power to save a few lost sailors stuck on their boat for a hundred years."

Hana pumped her fist in the air. "Damned straight."

Her fiancé frowned slightly before he continued. "I wasn't able to find any direct photographs of the ship, only fuzzy outlines of questionable provenance. The few magical witnesses who happened to see it also report that there is some kind of distortion field around the shield that appears magical in nature and interfered with their spells. Because of that, no one has been able to directly verify the registry ID numbers.

"You told me to avoid drawing the government's attention, so I haven't poked around in their records to see if I could confirm that a USS *Constantinople* even existed. Depending on how thorough they were in erasing it from history, that might not be possible to do in the time we have remaining. The only thing I can say for certain is that a ship has definitely appeared on and off on Halloween throughout the decades, and it appears to be a World War II-era destroyer escort."

He acts like finding all that out is no big deal, but if anything, he's made me more determined to do this.

The fox blew a raspberry. "Come on. Most ghost ships are old-timey, right? Like sails and stuff. The one people have seen has to be the one from Hawaii. There can't be too many different dark, secret magical experiments people attempted on Navy ships in World War II, can there?"

Ava cleared her throat tentatively. "If I might interject, Miss Brownstone? I have some information relevant to the discussion. It won't, perhaps, provide as much clarity as you would like, but it's not useless either."

Alison nodded. "Go ahead. Anything you can share would be appreciated."

Why am I not surprised that she knows something?

"There was an unusually strong magical anomaly detected in the Pacific on Halloween in 1943. The timing of the event does correspond with the evening in the Hawaii-Aleutian Time Zone. The exact location of the anomaly couldn't be determined at the time, but it was in the vicinity of the Hawaiian islands."

Hana pointed at the woman. "See. It's real. It's the *Constantinople.*"

Her boss didn't bother to ask where she obtained the information. The important thing was that she had shared it. All the pieces were falling together to confirm this wasn't merely a legend in the Latherby family and that there was a physical vessel they could track.

"Can you tell us anything else?" she asked. "Anything you might have heard, even if it doesn't seem immediately important."

Ava nodded. "The magicals in the UK government at the time, through back channels, attempted to convince the US government magicals to explain what had happened. There had been general cooperation in terms of the mild amount of magic tolerated during the war, and there was concern that it was some kind of secret Japanese magical attack the Americans were too afraid to admit had happened—a magical Pearl Harbor if you will. The US refused to clarify the details and merely stated that there had been a magical accident. They insisted that they were coordinating with the Silver Griffins, among others, to handle the aftermath and assured everyone that there would be no exposure of magic to the outside world. The UK government was rebuffed when they attempted to go directly to the Griffins."

Alison uttered a little snort. "The Griffins? Yeah, that's inconvenient for us. It's not like there are any of them around we can chat to about it. Even most of their artifacts were scattered. My mom ran into more than a few, though." She ran a hand through her hair and down to her neck. "Why do I have the feeling that whoever did this magical experiment screwed up badly and then decided it was too much trouble to save the men themselves? I doubt they even tried to save them and instead, told everyone they were dead to not look bad or risk exposing the magical world."

Hana shuddered. "Do you really think they would let them suffer like that?"

"Things are different these days. You and I never knew a time without magic, but back then, everyone did their best on both planets to hide it. I can totally see the magicals in the government deciding it was an acceptable loss rather than stirring up trouble. They were playing fast and loose with the rules as it was to perform those kinds of experiments around and with so many non-magicals. Everyone was supposed to be careful about the magic but with a war on, it gave them an excuse to do nasty things and know that almost everything could be explained away if a building was blown up in a battle. You should hear some of the stories my mom has turned up in her research. Some of it is chilling, and on both sides."

"Perfect," Drysi mumbled. "The most annoying secrets are the ones people tried to bury a long time ago. I don't know if that means this is safer or more dangerous."

Something approaching discomfort played across Ava's face. "There's one more thing, Miss Brownstone. Despite this being a magical incident, certain agencies—both American and British—who were more focused on non-Oriceran extraterrestrials, along with their descendant agencies, also displayed an interest in the Pacific anomaly."

Alison stared at the woman for a moment. Her assistant had revealed before that she was still in contact with people from her mysterious prior life but had never demonstrated that she could contact them on such short notice. She hadn't even told her about the job until a couple of hours before.

The Welsh witch frowned. "If fucking alien hunters want this, maybe we should stay the hell away from it. For all we know, we'll walk into something nasty. I know those Nine Systems Alliance bastards don't have magic, but the Tapestry proved that simply because you're not from Oriceran or Earth doesn't mean you don't have access to magical power. How do we counter magic we've never encountered?"

Hana growled. "We did with those Tapestry assholes." She punched her palm. "I'm not scared of any weird aliens, even if they aren't pet thieves."

Tahir gave Drysi a look of slight disapproval. Alison wasn't sure if it was because she'd upset his girlfriend or if he didn't approve of her logic.

"There have been no odd inhuman creatures associated with the previous sightings," he explained. "While there are rumors associated with that kind of thing with the original Philadelphia Experiment cover story, the preponderance of the evidence points away from it being anything other than normal magic. The interest of alien hunters might be incidental."

Alison almost laughed. She was a half-Drow princess who traveled between two worlds. Now, she discussed aliens and magic with her staff and none of that seemed odd or unusual at all. Sometimes, she wondered what it would have been like to have grown up in a world where magic was considered a fairy tale. She'd already grown up in a world where space aliens were considered something only cranks believed in and she'd accepted it without much trouble.

"I've heard versions of the Philadelphia Experiment story that mention aliens," she said, "but I always assumed they were merely misinterpreting magic like they had in most cases. Tahir could be right and the alien hunters were merely poking around to be thorough."

"We could try to get a hold of NOAT," Hana suggested. "Ophelia seemed cool. She might give us more info."

Mason grunted in disapproval. "She might not have tried to lock us up but she's still a CIA agent and part of a group that continues to hide the truth about aliens. At the end of the day, NOAT cares more about keeping a lid on aliens than it does anything else. We can't trust them or her."

Drysi nodded at him. "Even if it's not aliens, whoever ran the magical boat went out of their way to bury this.

That means they had their reasons, and even over a hundred years later, they told Latherby to back the fuck off. If we stick our noses into it, we might piss the government off."

Hana squared her shoulders. "Let 'em target us. The government should know better than to mess with a Brownstone by now. If not, they might need a reminder."

Alison shook her head quickly. "We won't start a fight with the government if we can help it, but to the best of my knowledge, Agent Latherby was the only one told to not look into this. If we don't go out of our way to announce it, they shouldn't even arrive on our doorstep to ask. The only person who knows about the job other than us is Latherby, and he has all the reason in the world to keep his mouth shut."

Tahir nodded. "I haven't come across any reports of government-affiliated agents harassing any witnesses nor any indications of particular regulations or laws issued against it. That makes sense. How do you pass a law telling someone not to investigate a ship that allegedly doesn't even exist?"

"Well, there we go." Alison nodded. "There's no law against hunting ghost ships. We're in the clear."

The witch sighed, her deep incredulity all but painted on her face in neon colors. "Let me be damned clear on this. We'll take a job to find a fucking ghost ship—one the American government doesn't want us to find—and we have no idea what might be aboard it. For all we know, it might contain a tentacled demon that feeds on souls and on top of it, we won't even be paid by the client."

When she says it like that, it does sound bad.

She took a deep breath and her expression turned determined. "I don't know if the sailors on that ship are stuck halfway to the World in Between or somewhere else entirely, but I've heard enough stories from Berens women about how much that experience can suck." Her expression darkened. "If Latherby is right—and I have every reason to believe he is—what we do know is that ship will come to Earth on Halloween. It might be the only chance to save anyone for years, and I want to help those men. I understand what you're saying, Drysi, and if necessary, I'm willing to do this alone. I know there are considerable dangers involved and I won't order anyone to help me. I'm asking my friends and won't hold it against anyone who doesn't want to be involved."

She inclined her head at Tahir. "Given what we've heard about magical disruption, we probably won't have contact with the outside and this isn't a job Latherby's even paying for. So, we'll go without our infomancer support on a job in the middle of the ocean somewhere. I also understand this is nothing but self-satisfaction on my part and that not everyone wants to play hero. If you want to help, I can pay out bonuses. But if you choose not to, I'll respect that."

Mason groaned and scrubbed a hand down his face. "I know that stubborn look, A. There's nothing I can do to talk you out of this, is there?"

She shook her head. "Nope. I might not be able to save those men but I'll definitely give it my best attempt."

"Of course, there's no way I'll let my wife board a ghost ship by herself." He managed a grin. "The last thing I need to do is try to start a new relationship with ghost Alison arriving every few years to glare at me."

"You're likely correct about being blocked from the outside," Tahir interjected, "but I'll do my best to support you if possible."

"I was sold from the beginning and am on board with this." Hana grinned. "I kind of like the idea of playing hero. It's full circle—con woman to hot fox who saves sailors or frees their ghost spirits. Whatever works. It's all the same to me even if I don't have a cool hero name."

Drysi sighed. "It's not like I can back out now, and we both know I've done enough in my life that I owe the world a few favors and will long after I'm dead. I only wanted to make sure I knew what kind of fucking madness I would agree to."

Alison smiled around the table. "We have a few days before Halloween. From what Latherby told me, we'll have a narrow window. We have no idea where it'll appear, so we'll have to see if there's any change in the music box. If there isn't by sundown our time, we'll try to search. For the next few days, relax. I want you rested for our Halloween ghost hunt." She pointed to her phone. "And we all should memorize what Ensign Latherby looks like. If he's dead, we can at least ID the body and let the agent know."

CHAPTER SEVEN

Halloween's twilight settled over Seattle. The sky was clear to provide twinkling stars and a bright moon to shine on the costumed children who wandered the streets and the actual magical creatures that now inhabited the city. Most of the Brownstone employees had already gone home, but the magical team, along with Ava, waited in the conference room and made the final checks on their gear. The music box rested in front of Alison and taunted her with its silence.

If we wait here all night for nothing, I'll feel like an idiot, but Latherby's not the kind of guy who operates off hope and a prayer. This can't be a wild goose chase. Wild ghost goose chase?

Hana ran her hand along the *tachi* sheath that rested atop the conference room table. "We should have brought Omni instead of sending him home with Tahir. He can probably eat ghosts, even if they're alien ghosts. He can kill normal aliens."

"I doubt he can eat ghosts," her fiancé replied, his voice coming through the small receiver in her ear. "He does seem a little pensive, but he's an iguana right now and always seems pensive in that form."

"Oh, my little scalebaby misses his mommy, is all."

"Perhaps."

Drysi stared at her vest filled with enchanted daggers. "I can't believe I'm doing this on Halloween. I can't be the only person who has had a shit encounter on Halloween. I know it had to be today, but I prefer my enemies to be the flesh and blood—the easy to blow up kind."

"I ran into weird stuff at the School of Necessary Magic on more than one Halloween," Alison admitted. "And a few other times after, but I'm much stronger than I was before. I'm not worried, especially this time."

The Welsh witch looked down for a moment before she raised her head and nodded. "I won't lie, I'm much stronger than my last annoying encounter too. My gun might inflict considerable damage, but I have a spell or two I'd love to try if that's what it comes down to."

Mason counted his pistol magazines before he slid them into a tactical vest. "What do we do if the sailors are all alive but they don't believe us? If we start going on about magic, they'll think we're crazy."

"The wizards can explain," Alison suggested.

"They might still find the explanation unacceptable or think we're Axis magical spies."

Hana winked. "I'll charm them all if I need to. Charmafox to the rescue."

The music box began to turn and a slow, haunting melody emerged. Magic began to radiate from the instrument.

Yes!

Hana grimaced. "Jeez, no wonder Latherby is the way he is if that's the kind of thing he's listened to for years. Couldn't they have chosen a happier song?"

"I don't care about the music. I only care about the fact that it's playing. We're now on the clock, people." Alison stood and clapped. "Is everyone ready? We'll use the joint tracking ritual we discussed this afternoon, combined with Tahir's help, with the music box as a focus. It's time to find the *Constantinople*."

"And if it doesn't work?" Mason snatched his wand from the table. "We've made far too many assumptions with this plan."

"Then we'll try a different ritual but if we can't find them, we can't find them. All we can do is try."

The fox leaned back in her chair and smiled. "Okay, get to it. Charmafox's powers are helpful, but not in this situation."

Ava stood. "I'll leave you to the magic. I have a few things to check on."

A half-hour later, Alison wiped the sweat off her brow. She'd had to shove a huge amount of power into what was usually a fairly easy type of magic. Mason and Drysi both breathed heavily, their hands clutched around their wands. Translucent circles of cerulean and scarlet spun around the music box. The spell was working.

"I have the coordinates," Tahir declared. "I've borrowed a few satellites to help, and I've verified that there is what appears to be a World War II-era escort destroyer surrounded by some kind of energy field in the Arctic Ocean north of British Colombia."

Hana wrinkled her nose. "That sounds...cold. Why couldn't they have chosen the Caribbean? Charmafox likes warm weather."

Drysi scoffed. "You live in Seattle."

The other woman shrugged. "It doesn't mean I can't like warm weather."

The conference room door opened. Ava wandered in with four white parkas draped over her arms.

Alison laughed. "Of course you'd be ready."

Sometimes, I wonder if she's more of a magical than she lets on. Or...maybe she's like Dad. That might explain why she knows so much about aliens and had to leave the UK in a hurry. Someday, maybe she'll tell me.

It didn't matter that her assistant had secrets. If she had a secret agenda of betrayal, she'd already passed up numerous opportunities. She trusted her implicitly, and the woman had risked her life to help her on more than one occasion.

Ava set the parkas on the table. "These should be helpful. I understand the tactical inconvenience, but please bundle up."

The fox sighed. "There's no decent way to look sexy in a parka. At least not with my body type."

"Priorities, Hana," Alison reminded her.

Drysi smirked. "Your man will be thousands of miles away. Who do you want to look sexy for?"

"My adoring public. It'll be a gift to those poor sailors after everything they've suffered—or at least it would be without the parka." Hana stood. She eyed the garment and then her sword belt. "I'm probably better off with this under it, but it's still annoying." She slipped her sword belt on.

A couple of minutes passed as the team donned their tactical vests and holsters and cast their baseline battle enchantments before they shrugged into the parkas but didn't zip them. They had no idea what they would encounter when they stepped foot on the ship and needed easy access to their wands, guns, and knives.

I hope the sailors don't think we're a group of crazy mercenaries.

"Is everyone ready?" Alison raised her hand. It was time to open a portal to the *Constantinople.*

Hana raised her arms and lowered her voice. "Boooooooo. Look at me. I'm a ghost."

Her boss frowned. "Show a little respect, Hana."

"Oh, lighten up. All these sailors will be super-happy when we find them and take them back to America, but a cool America in the future with magic and stuff. It'll be like a miracle." The fox grinned. "You'll see."

I won't point out that they'll have outlived all their families. We need to save them, but it'll be a hard adjustment for most of these guys.

Alison sighed. "Sure. Okay, Tahir, maybe we'll get lucky and still be able to chat to you on the other side. If it works, I can open a portal so you can get a drone through."

"One can hope," he replied. "But I'm dubious."

"Glass half-empty, huh?"

He smiled. "I'd say the same applies to you."

Mason tucked his wand into its holster. "Mongol

demon prisons and ghost Navy ships. Sometimes, I miss the simplicity that came with being a bodyguard."

"And sometimes I miss the simplicity of not knowing I was a magical." Alison took a few deep breaths before she uttered the portal enchantment. She manipulated the flows of light and shadow magic and tightened her shadow flows with compression as she focused on the magical connection their tracking ritual had established. Slight magical pressure pushed against her. She shoved even more magic into opening the portal while she attempted to hold the connection to the music box.

Come on. We can't fail now. Not when we're so damned close. I can do this—no, I will do this.

A portal juddered open in front of her and stabilized after a few seconds. A dense, glowing green fog lay on the other side.

"Okay, that's...different," Hana observed.

"We expected it to be strange," she replied. "And now, it's time to save the men. You all go first. It's taking a little more magic than I planned to keep this stable."

Mason frowned. "Different can also mean dangerous." He drew his weapon and stepped through. Hana readied her blade and followed, whistling a jaunty tune. Drysi walked behind her and muttered something in Welsh. Alison followed and let the portal snap shut behind her.

"Tahir?" she asked and tapped the receiver in her ear. "Can you hear me?"

There was no response.

With a sigh, she looked around as she removed the receiver and shoved it in her pocket. The glowing fog surrounded the ship and partially obscured a shimmering field of energy that extended farther in a rough dome. It pushed away the night's darkness with its eerie multi-hued light. They had arrived on the bow and she could make out only the barest outlines of the pilothouse and tower through the fog. A huge forward turret stood ahead of them, turned at a ninety-degree angle.

She frowned and licked her lips. No frigid winds cut at their face. Instead, the night air was balmy.

"Is it only me, or is it not that cold?"

Mason shed his parka and dropped it on the deck. "No. If we run around in these things, not only will they be obnoxious, we'll be sweating in five seconds."

"Ava can't always be right," Hana commented. "Even if she is probably a super-Mary Poppins alien-killing ninja knight."

Alison shrugged. "I don't think it's crazy to suggest heavy coats for the arctic in late October. And no one could have expected that it would be warm on this ship."

The women all removed their jackets. Drysi took a moment to recover a few magazines from the pockets and stowed them in her tactical vest.

"Trouble!" Hana tapped her crystal ring three times. A red glow suffused her skin. A moment later, she growled. Her nine tails of light appeared and her claws extended. She pointed her sword at the back of the turret.

The Drow summoned a shadow blade and looked in the indicated direction. A white-uniformed sailor lay partially fused into the turret. His face was frozen in a mask of terror but there was no sign of blood. He looked pale, especially under the mostly green light, but there was no sign of decay.

Mason retrieved his wand and chanted a spell. He frowned and chanted again before he shook his head. "He's completely dead—he's not breathing and has no heartbeat. But there's considerable interference with the spell. It's not like I couldn't cast it but more like the information was somehow scrambled."

"I hope that doesn't apply to battle magic." Alison advanced into the fog past the dead sailor. The team fell into a diamond formation, with Drysi in the rear and Mason and Hana on the flanks. They cleared the turret.

The fox shivered. "What a way to die." She sighed. "Poor guy. I'm so sorry."

It's not simply a fun ghost hunt now, is it?

"It's not your fault," Alison murmured.

A dozen more men were scattered in the immediate area. Most were fused into the deck or the railing, some by their arms and some head-first. Others looked like they'd fallen into quicksand and been stuck halfway. Exactly like the sailor in the turret, they all looked as if they'd died in terror and pain.

"This is awful." She grimaced. "I begin to see why they might have wanted to cover this up."

Hana sheathed her sword and shook her head. "I thought they were supposed to keep magic under control back then." Pity filled her eyes. "This is disgusting, and they didn't even know what was going on."

Drysi scoffed. "There was a war on. History teaches that if there's a weapon available, people will use it, even if they're not supposed to. All the pompous veneer of the Griffins and other bastards didn't mean much. It's not like there weren't any number of rogue wizards who caused problems even before the gates opened." She gestured to a dead sailor. "And I don't know if this counts as rogue wizards."

Mason raised his wand to check for any survivors in the area. He shook his head. "Exactly like the other one. They're all dead. And there is still a fair amount of interference, but I understand how to deal with it better."

"The bodies all look totally fresh, although pale," Alison observed. "If it were cold here, it'd make sense that the bodies might be preserved, but it's been over a hundred years. Shouldn't they be a little nastier than that?

"Maybe, A. But this is all magic. I don't really know if physical reality matters. The magic might have wiped out all the microbes that contribute to it."

"But there should still be some signs." She knelt near a middle-aged sailor who was neatly separated into an almost perfect half above the deck with the rest of his body presumably fused into the metal. "They also might not show any signs of decay because they haven't been here that long."

The Welsh witch frowned. "What are you saying? That the spell sent them through time? I don't know if that's even possible. I've not heard of actual time travel magic."

"After all the things I've dealt with in my life, including Dad and the Tapestry, I'm no longer sure what's possible." She stood. "It's only a theory, but if it's right, it means we have a better chance to find survivors. It might not have been hundreds of men trying to survive a century. It might be a handful of sailors after the initial accident merely trying to stay calm for a couple of hours after they witnessed this bizarre horror."

"Look around, Alison. These poor bastards are all dead." Drysi clenched a hand into a fist. "Some fucking wizards got it into their head that they would develop a nice, tidy spell to help win the war, and all they did was kill their own men. Right now, I wish I could find them so I could put a bullet in their fucking heads."

I'm not so sure I disagree. They experimented on these men. Even if the war was on, the crew didn't deserve this.

Alison sighed. "Latherby said his great-grandfather had issues with the experiment. He might have suspected something like this would happen. I hope he tried to do the right thing."

Hana sniffed the air. "It's hard to tell with all the over-lapping magic blocking everything, but there's a faint scent that might be a human."

"That might be left over from them." Mason gestured toward one of the bodies.

"I can't be sure." The fox shrugged.

A distant loud clang sounded and a massive wave of magic passed through them.

Alison's stomach tightened and bile rose in the back of her throat. "I'm not the only one who felt that, right?"

Drysi gritted her teeth. "What if we end up fused to the floor? I won't lie. I've thought about all kinds of gruesome ways I might die and that wasn't one of them."

"We won't," she insisted. She pointed her sword down. "But from what I felt, there's a major source of magic deeper in the ship. If there's magic, there might be survivors, either the wizards or men with the wizards."

"And you want to find the bastard wizards who did this?"

"Maybe." Her gaze lingered on a dead sailor. "If they survived, they need to answer for what they've done, but check all the bodies as best you can. See if you can find Abner Latherby."

The grim work continued for a couple of minutes, at least on the bodies with exposed faces and heads. None of them belonged to the ensign.

"Should we cut the ship open and check those with their heads in the metal?" Drysi asked. Her tone was apologetic. Even a hardened killer could have respect for the dead.

Alison shook her head. "Not yet. I think we should move toward whatever was responsible for that magic we felt."

"Not the bridge?"

"No, we need to go where the magic is, and it didn't seem to come from there." She gestured vaguely in the direction of the pilothouse. When she looked closer, she realized the ship was missing its radio masts.

Hana raised a clawed hand. "I do want to point out that this is the part in every horror movie where you're, like, 'No, no, don't go toward the monster, you idiot.'"

Shadows coalesced into wings behind Alison's back. She maintained them for a few seconds before she released them.

"I'm a Dark Elf princess. You're a nine-tailed fox, and we have a wizard and a witch with us. We don't have to worry about monsters. Compared to who we'll probably run into, we're the monsters."

The woman glanced at her claws and turned her head

to smile at her tails. "Okay, that's a fair point. Charmafox can be too much when people first meet her."

The Drow pointed to a nearby hatch barely visible in the glowing fog. "Let's try to go down without breaking anything first. We might still be able to bring the entire ship back and we don't want to risk hurting someone."

"And if we don't find anyone alive?" Drysi asked.

"Then we think about sinking the ship," she suggested. She craned her head up and narrowed her eyes to try to make out more details of the magical field surrounding the vessel. Her focus seemed to find nothing but stars and the moon. "At least we can give them a burial of sorts that way."

CHAPTER EIGHT

Mason twisted the hatch and pulled it open while everyone else held weapons at the ready. No monsters emerged, thankfully. The only sight was a slick series of ladder stairs that extended into a narrow passage. The green fog within swirled low and grew thicker along the passageway deeper inside to provide sinister illumination.

How many horrors like this are lost to history?

Alison conjured a light orb before she layered a shield over herself and summoned a new shadow blade. If she wanted to save anyone, she needed to make sure she survived. She descended the stairs and noticed another poor sailor embedded in a bulkhead near the bottom. At least this one had his eyes closed. The light thump of the others stepping down the stairs echoed down the corridor.

Another pulse of magic rippled through the area and every color in the room shifted. A rainbow riot of patches of varying shades suffused the space. The fog changed in hue and density. For a moment, a bulkhead began to vanish. A stream of different smells struck Alison—sweet, rancid, and earthy—and a beautiful melody was followed by a sharp, dissonant cry.

Vertigo struck her and she fell to one knee. The bizarre distortion stopped. Everything returned to what had been before. No one could call the status quo normal, but at least it didn't challenge their basic senses.

"What the fuck was that?" Drysi asked.

Hana growled.

Alison took a deep breath and stood. "Whatever magic they used still seems to affect everything. We need to find the source." She strode forward while bile rose in the back of her throat.

Hana's right. They were supposed to control all this, but they let this crap happen. This isn't someone smuggling magic in under the noses of the Griffins. This is hundreds of men who didn't even know why they died. It's strange distortions in reality.

She ground her teeth. Everything in her wanted to find the wizards responsible—not to save them but to drag them back for punishment if she didn't deliver it herself, even if that included Abner Latherby.

A low groan reverberated through the corridor and the bulkheads bowed slightly as if something was squeezing them. The fog swirled together in different places and thinned as it did so.

The Drow lifted her blade. "This doesn't look good."

"Is it the ghosts of the crew?" Hana asked as her grasp tightened around her *tachi*. "We're here to help you," she called.

Alison gestured for them to move forward. Now that the fog didn't obscure the entire passage, they could see farther down, including several dead sailors. Unlike those they had found before, the men had clearly been torn apart. Bloodstains covered the floor and nearby bulkheads.

Drysi yanked an explosive dagger out before she sheathed it with a frown. "That's probably not the best choice in tight quarters." She yanked her wand out instead.

"Probably," her boss agreed.

The swirling fog thickened into solid forms. Five-legged monsters took shape with dark jointed limbs and something that vaguely resembled arms with sharp and flat bone-like protrusions from the end. Their dark orb-like bodies lacked any distinguishing features that might mark sensory organs. Each beast was short, only a few feet in height.

"Yeah, this is less than fine. And it's probably useless to chat but I have to try. Just because they look weird doesn't mean they're evil. They could simply be rude like a Halican." She took a deep breath. "I'm Alison Brownstone," she called. "We're not here to fight but to rescue any humans who might have survived."

The fog cleared completely and formed into eight of the creatures. They remained motionless for a couple of seconds and almost looked like shadows under the bright light of her orb.

Okay, maybe I have something viable here. If they are only strange creatures who were caught up in this mess like the sail—

The monsters broke into a scuttling attack with their arm blades raised.

Okay, maybe not.

Alison lashed out with her arm and launched a shadow crescent. The spell sliced halfway through one of the monsters and the wounded beast spilled a black fluid onto the floor. The wound slowed it but didn't stop its progress. Mason opened fire with his pistol. His target jerked as the bullets blew large holes into the monster. Again, the injuries slowed but didn't halt it. Drysi didn't attack immediately. She murmured a quiet spell under her breath and held her wand pointed down the passageway. A few more shadow crescents sliced one of the monsters in half. Its pieces fell and the legs and arms twitched. Hana growled and sheathed the *tachi* quickly. She drew her gun and opened fire.

The witch's wand glowed brightly. A wrenching groan issued from the walls. Metal pulled from the nearby bulkheads and twisted into a giant net around the monsters. Boxes spilled from the holes formed on either side and toppled on top of the trap. The creatures thrashed and scraped against their prison but the metal didn't give.

Her boss grinned. "Nice thinking. I get too used to overwhelming power."

"Not all of us are Drow princesses." The woman twirled her wand in her fingers. "And we're far enough away from the sides of the ship that I thought it wouldn't end with the ocean pouring in."

"Yeah, that would suck. For now, let's eliminate these." The Drow channeled magic into smaller purple-tinged dark orbs. She held her hands up and they launched into the net to annihilate any trapped monsters they struck.

Drysi put her wand away and retrieved her gun to join

Mason and Hana who had already begun to fire. The black ichor inside the creatures splattered over the boxes and metal crates nearby. If the team hadn't fought bizarre aberrations before, it might have been troubling, but for the moment, it was merely another obstacle between them and the strong source of magic they still felt. The pile of legs and bladed arms that had once been the enemy continued to twitch. A rancid smell wafted from the carnage.

Hana sighed. "Too bad Ava didn't think to give me a mask." She wrinkled her nose. "And please tell me I'm not the only one suffering from the smell."

Alison shook her head. "No, it's not only you. That smells awful."

Mason pointed to a door directly in front of the net. "We should be able to go through there and round the back through the hole Drysi made in the room."

"Be careful." She advanced in the front of the team, her shadow sword ready. "So the people who didn't end up fused to the ship had to deal with the fog turning into monsters? It must have been too quick for them to even do anything."

She opened the door and crept inside. Boxes and wooden crates filled the small room. One cracked crate lay on its side and a small mountain of potatoes had fallen out. She looked to her side. Crates and boxes filled the other room, along with long gray lidded boxes. A small puddle of water surrounded one.

Freezers, maybe? It doesn't matter if there's no one in there.

The team continued through the supply room past the trapped, twitching remnants of the monsters until they rejoined the main passage. A closed door with a large round handle stood at the end of it.

Alison released her sword and spun the warm, slick handle slowly. "Is everyone ready? There might be more of those inside."

"We should have simply blown a hole in the damned thing and let it sink," Drysi grumbled.

CHAPTER NINE

When Alison pulled open the door, there was no fog in the room. Nor were there any fused bodies or monsters. Metal tables filled the cramped area, all welded directly into the deck. Padded seats extended from the tables. Thin metal beams ran from the deck to the ceiling in several places and a long metal island stood off to the side, bolted directly into the deck. Several bunks protruded from the other side of the room, and large hooks hung from the ceiling in several places. A huge firehose was mounted on the wall.

Everything about the ship was incredibly cramped. She couldn't imagine what it would have been like to have to live on a vessel like the *Constantinople* for months at a time.

And I used to sometimes feel like I didn't have enough space at the School of Necessary Magic.

Hana eyed the bunks. "It's kind of a strange setup. Isn't this the cafeteria?"

"Yes, but I think it's called a mess," Mason explained. "From what I understand, they would cook the food elsewhere and bring it here, but they sometimes needed additional space for sailors. It's not uncommon in this kind of ship and especially in this period, but I don't know about more modern ships."

"Your bedroom's in the cafeteria. Yeah, that would suck." The fox sighed. "No one's here, though. Wouldn't there be a few guys getting a sandwich or something when things went down?"

"Why would they be?" Alison asked. "The magical nature of the experiment might have been secret from most of the crew, but they still would have had them ready in case anything went wrong. It would be all hands on deck or battle stations or whatever they do in the Navy. They wouldn't have had guys anywhere but at their normal workstations."

"That makes sense. I only—" The woman spun toward a table and uttered a low growl, her tails suddenly rigid. She drew her sword. A pair of boots protruded, the full body obscured by the surface from their present angle.

The Drow summoned a new shadow blade and crept forward. A man lay under the table, his eyes fixed in a death stare. Like everyone else on the ship, he wore a white Naval uniform, but unlike everyone else they had seen, he clutched an oak wand in his right hand. A jagged tear sliced through his chest, and blood stained the front of his uniform.

"It's a dead wizard," she said quickly. "Not Abner Latherby, though."

"Does it fucking matter?" Drysi muttered. "Even a wizard's dead. I think we have to face it, Alison. I don't think anyone survived this. I feel sorry for the poor bastards, but this ship is surrounded by a magic fog that turns into monsters and we've not heard anyone. It's not like we're quiet, either. If someone was hiding, you'd think they'd come out to wave down all the talking people."

Hana looked around the cramped room and gestured with her sword. "But we took out those monsters with a little magic and guns. They have guns on these ships, right?"

"They do," Alison confirmed. "But I haven't seen any. If it happened too quickly, perhaps they didn't have time to get them. They might not have wanted anyone to carry one during the experiment, either. This is a military ship that was active during World War II. People obeyed orders."

Mason frowned. "They also didn't expect to be attacked. The wizards might have even fed everyone a line about a light show. If what Agent Latherby said is correct, they probably hoped to teleport the ship to a new place and then teleport it back. It's not like they would want to stick around somewhere they didn't control. Magic's helpful, but it might not save them from a Japanese battleship."

She continued to study the body and wondered what had gone through the wizard's mind in the last few minutes of his life. Did he feel guilt or had he been merely afraid?

"There's still that magic we can all sense," she said finally. "And we haven't confirmed that everyone's dead. We also had that strange reality distortion wave."

"I would try to check for life signs all over," Mason commented, "but there's so much interference, it won't do much good. We'd need to go room to room."

Drysi sighed and rubbed her temples. "I hate this ghost

monster shit, but I'd hate to be a poor bastard who survived and was left behind after someone came to rescue his ass. We might not be able to check the entire ship, but we can at least check the source of magic."

Alison pulled her phone out.

Hana laughed. "Do you actually think you'll get reception? If my man can't connect to us, no phone company can." She rolled her eyes and rested a hand on her hip.

She shook her head. "I don't care about reception. I care about the time. According to this, it's been less than thirty minutes since we arrived and about an hour since we performed the ritual."

Mason shrugged. "That sounds about right."

"Did you notice anything about those storerooms?" She gestured toward the door they'd entered through.

"Sailors really like potatoes?" the fox suggested. "Or they hate potatoes and the Navy gives them to sailors as a punishment."

"There was no hint that anything had rotted, exactly like the bodies we've found. I'm not sure if that means there's nothing here to help that process along or if there's something weird going on with time."

Drysi scraped her boot against the floor. "How would we know if there was something wrong with time? If we're inside the effect of the spell, we'd experience it the same way the sailors did."

"You're right, and I'm not sure." She looked from the dead wizard to her friends. While she wanted to help anyone left on board, she now worried about being stuck in a strange alternate dimension or the World in Between. It might not be impossible to escape but it came damned close, which was why the Oricerans still liked to use it as a last resort for dangerous magical criminals.

Mason looked uneasy before he steeled his features. "Whatever the hell is going on here is one thing, but we do know the *Constantinople* stays visible until sunrise, right? Even with the fog and the field earlier, it was still obviously nighttime."

"You're right. We could see the moon and the stars. Let's go back to the main deck and check the sky. If it still looks dark, we'll retrace our steps to minimize new attacks." Alison gestured to Hana's sword. "I hate to tell you this, but it might be better to use your gun and claws when we're inside the ship. That is too big to swing in most of these cramped little rooms."

The fox sheathed her sword with an overdramatic flourish. "Whatever you say, boss."

For all the drama that came with their initial entry below deck, the hurried return to the main deck proceeded without incident. The fog outside still clung to the *Constantinople,* but it swirled away from them as they neared it, almost as if it were afraid. The glow and the light of the field surrounding the ship and even Hana's tails pushed the night back, but stars still hung in the sky and looked as numerous as they had before. It was an imperfect way to judge the passage of time, but given that they were on a Navy ship, it felt appropriate in a way.

Was that magic earlier a wizard's SOS?

A hurried descent brought them to the mess, and a trip

through another door connected to that placed them in a room filled with sinks and racks of dishes—a scullery, obviously, although they couldn't see anything unusual. They did, however, seem to move closer to the source of the magic. There was no sign of any new fog and hadn't been since they re-entered the ship. Cautiously, they moved from the scullery into a passage. There were a few doors to each side but it ended in another sealed door. The intense magic pressure was unmistakable.

"I think we found the source," Alison announced. "There could be survivors in there or there could be an unimaginable horror ready to eat us."

"Then what's the plan?" Drysi asked. "Being eaten is another way I'd prefer not to die."

"I think we should knock," Hana suggested and raised her claws. "Monsters don't knock. If there are people inside, they'll understand that we're people, too."

"That's fine by me," her boss said, moved toward the door, and raised her hand. "Everyone, back up and be ready in case this turns dangerous."

Mason chuckled. He pulled his wand out and chanted a quick spell to refresh his barely visible shields. Hana and Drysi raised their guns while they retreated a few steps.

Alison banged loudly and waited. There was no response. She tried again with no better success.

"Okay, it's time to open it then." She released her shadow blade and began to turn the door handle. Determination pushed any concern aside. She wouldn't leave the ship without answers, and that strange magic had only raised more questions.

"Woah, A, shouldn't you keep your blade ready?" Mason asked.

She shook her head and channeled energy into her legs. "If a monster comes out, I'll jump back. You guys can eliminate it and I'll counterattack. Does that sound good?"

"I think this kind of thing's more fun with a talking dog and a guy in an ascot," Hana mumbled.

Alison had no idea what she had referenced and decided to leave it alone. She turned the handle until she heard a soft clank. "Is everyone ready?"

Her team nodded and pointed their weapons at the door. She pushed it open.

"Okay, I didn't quite expect that," she commented.

A yard ahead of her, an opaque wall of blue energy extended from floor to ceiling.

Hana shrugged. "At least it's not another creepy monster."

CHAPTER TEN

"That explains why no one responded to the knocking." Alison gestured to the blue magical wall. "I don't know if they can hear through that."

The large compartment, even near the front, was a maze of pipes and tubes running into massive long pieces of gray machinery on either side of a narrow aisle. It was larger than most of the sections they'd been in, including the crew mess. The machines were covered in multiple closed sections with access panels. The blue field cut through the equipment. Various gauges covered the nearby wall, their needles all to one side or the other.

She summoned another light orb and directed it across the room. All the machinery blocked much of the light from her first orb, which left far too many shadowed corners for her comfort.

Despite the impressive equipment, there wasn't any noise in the room other than the sound of their breathing and the scuff of their boots. The room was dead, exactly like everything else on the *Constantinople*.

Maybe Drysi's right and no one made it. For all I know, the government already sent magicals here and realized the horror and decided there was nothing they could do about it. Did they seal something off?

"What are those things?" Hana asked and gestured to one of the machines. "Are those torpedo tubes or depth charges or some other big Navy boom-boom thing?"

"I haven't a clue," Alison admitted. "I actually regret not studying the layout of this kind of ship more carefully before coming. I thought it'd be more of a situation where we arrived and everyone cheered, I opened a portal, and they all walked out."

Drysi tilted her head and a satisfied smile appeared. "They're engines. I love it."

They all turned toward her with surprised expressions.

She shrugged. "I might know shit about boats, but I know about fixing bikes so I know an engine when I see one, even if it's a big-ass one on a boat. I'm very sure these are diesel engines."

Hana wrinkled her nose. "Oh, is that what else I've smelled? I don't think I'd last long in the Navy, and not only because of their seriously non-sexy uniforms."

The witch approached some of the gauges. Her gaze darted to each of them in turn. "According to these, this ship is as dead as every man we've found so far. Poor bastards."

The fox edged toward the field with a frown and sniffed. "The magic from this doesn't smell like the other magic."

"It's only a magical barrier," Alison explained. "It's

strong magic but not overwhelming. There's no way it's responsible for what we've sensed. There's something behind it."

"It could be blocking a portal," Mason suggested with a frown. "It might be where those weird monsters came from. The wizards might have sealed it in with this."

"Why isn't there fog around here then?" Hana asked. "Isn't the fog the monsters?"

The Drow walked closer to the barrier. "You saw what happened earlier. It's like the fog's alive and it's too afraid to come near us." She paced along the shield in an effort to see if there were any obvious differences in the appearance of the field, but she couldn't find any. "Then again, if this is supposed to seal monsters in, it's obviously done a poor job judging by the creatures we fought. The fog's avoiding us for now, but it might come back." She stepped back, her brow furrowed in thought. Magical shields didn't go up for no reason, but she'd come too far to simply turn and leave.

"I can let you through," a man's voice said, seemingly from everywhere. "But the second I drop this spell, they'll come, and it'll take me a good thirty seconds to a minute to get it up again. It has to be tuned a certain way for reasons I don't want to go into right now."

"We fought our way through those monsters already," Alison responded. "We're all magicals with fighting experience. We've come to help the survivors on this ship." She paused for a moment and added a quick lie wrapped around a core of truth. "We were sent by the government."

Agent Latherby's technically a government agent.

"I assumed you were magicals," the man stated. "I doubt

non-magicals sent by the government would travel so freely with a fox demon."

Hana scoffed. "That's nine-tailed fox to you."

"We don't have time to argue, woman. I'm about to drop the field. There are some things we need to discuss but first, we need to be safe for a few minutes."

Alison turned toward the doorway. "Can the monsters go through walls?"

"No, thank God," he replied. "If you're talking about the sailors, it wasn't the monsters that did that. It was more the two-legged kind."

"Why not simply make a wall of metal?" the fox suggested. "We stopped them before with kind of a net of metal."

"I wish you hadn't done that." The man sighed. "This ship is barely hanging together as is. I'm sure you've seen the bodies. The structure was compromised by the spell. Several lower deck compartments are already flooded because one of my associates had a similar idea. If we start taking things apart too much, who knows what will happen? The entire ship could sink."

Drysi grimaced. "Damn. I could have killed us all."

"Hey, it worked, and you didn't. You had good intentions and it brought good results." Alison shrugged. "If we can't do it the easy way, we'll have to rely on the semi-easy way."

Mason, Drysi, and Hana all raised their guns.

She shook her head. "Hey, wizard behind the curtain, I have a question for you. We killed the monsters earlier with only a few easy spells and guns—those five-legged creatures with no faces. Are they all that weak?"

His response came as a bitter laugh. "If it were that easy, do you think I would be hiding behind here?"

Alison raised her palm. "Is there any ammo stored near here?"

"No."

"Good." She nodded at Drysi and Mason. "We should still limit the explosions in case, but we can open things up a little more."

The witch grinned. "There are many ways to kill something without explosions."

Their leader turned to Hana. "You stay near the door and slice any that get past us."

"Good." The fox drew her blade. "I haven't been able to use this baby yet."

The blue field vanished. A harried-looking wizard with a cherrywood wand stood farther back in the passage between the two engines. There were tears in his uniform, along with blood splatters. Another blue field remained behind him. His young face was identical to the picture the agent had provided. The man before them was Ensign Abner Latherby.

An array of shimmering crystals floated well beyond the engines. They orbited and pulsated, covered with twining streams of light. The patterns emitted reminded her of the field surrounding the ship. Intense magical pressure emanated from the array.

We found the source and Old Latherby, even if he's younger than his great-grandson.

Abner gestured for them to move closer. Drysi and Mason positioned themselves near one engine, and Alison beside the other. Hana stood to the side of the open door, a huge grin on her face and her sword held tightly. The glowing fog billowed into the passage and thickened with each passing second.

Does it want those crystals more than it fears us?

The ensign pointed his wand forward and began a rapid incantation in what sounded like a combination of Latin and Enochian. Particles of light swirled around the tip of his wand.

The fog coalesced into new monsters, both the strange five-legged beasts from before and others, including crystalline wormlike creatures over a yard long and covered in sharp spines. Ghostly humanoid shapes moved forward with juddering steps. Four-legged creatures that looked like they were composed of solid shadow joined the army.

The bizarre menagerie didn't worry her. It was the normal-looking creatures that emerged that made her heart race. In a fight full of horrors, why were gerbils attacking her?

It's not a big deal. They are probably the ones that feeds on souls.

Alison layered magic around a light orb and thrust the concentrated magic forward. The spell careened through the narrow space and burrowed through one of the crystal worms. The creature writhed and vaporized into thick gray smoke. A swirling purple beam erupted from Drysi's wand after an incantation in Welsh and carved through one of the five-legged monsters. An ice spear struck one of the gerbils. It exploded in a cloud of bright yellow liquid that splattered and sizzled on the metal of the floor and walls and carved a few gouges before it vaporized. Some of the monsters nearby fell and their bodies disintegrated under the deadly gerbil acid shower, including a shadow wolf.

Exploding acid gerbils. Of course.

One of the pentapods, as Alison had come to think of the five-legged monsters, reached the engine room. Hana rewarded it by chopping it in half and kicked its twitching legs into the passage.

"Keep them busy for a few seconds," their leader shouted. "I have another idea of how to slow them without sinking the ship." She began to make a few careful motions with her hands while she chanted a spell. Drysi's Welsh death ray attacks continued and she obliterated a worm and an acid gerbil. Mason continued to pelt the enemy with ice lances. Most succumbed but some were only slowed.

She finished her spell. A gust of wind whirled into the narrow passage. It struck the advancing monster horde and launched them back. She continued to feed magic into the spell and a grin built with each target that tumbled in her new wind tunnel. The only creatures unaffected by her attack were the juddering specters, which continued their slow, relentless advance.

Drysi and Mason fired at one, but their volleys simply passed through them.

"That's fucking annoying," the Welsh witch snarled.

A bright blue barrier field erupted from the floor and extended a few inches into the passageway.

Hana yelped and jumped back. She sniffed for a moment and grinned before she sheathed her blade, reverted to human form, and stretched. "I finally had a chance to use my sword on this job."

Alison turned to Abner. "And it's stable for now?"

"Yes, ma'am. It holds out any of those weird creatures and a few other things that I'll explain in a moment." He wiped the sweat from his brow. "I want to make one thing clear. The only reason I agreed to that crazy stunt is because you all seem like you know what you're doing and I'll need magical help for what I have planned." He frowned at her. "You seem like you're in charge, miss." He studied her warily. "Are you some kind of spy or something? OSS? I know they've recruited a few magicals to help them."

"I'm more an 'or something,' but yeah, I'm in charge. My name is Alison Brownstone." She gestured to her friends. "This is my husband, Mason, and these two are my friends and employees, Drysi Jones and Hana Sugimoto."

The wizard's gaze lingered on the fox for a moment, faint confusion on his face.

"You're not a witch, are you, Mrs. Brownstone?" He pointed to his wand. "I didn't see you using a wand and you have some strange help."

"I'm a half-Drow."

"I never met a Dark Elf before." He shrugged. "No offense, but I haven't heard great things."

She shrugged. "They're kind of under new management."

Abner chuckled. "I'm Ensign Abner Latherby of the United States Navy. Don't sugarcoat it for me, Mrs. Brownstone."

Wait. Mrs. Brownstone? Never mind, that's not important to correct.

"Sugarcoat what?" she asked.

He tucked his wand into his pocket and a weary look settled over his face. "How many years have passed since 1943?"

CHAPTER ELEVEN

"You realized that already?" Alison asked. She'd made the mistake of thinking that simply because he was a man of the previous century, he'd be slower to understand the concept.

People weren't any stupider back then, and this guy's still a wizard. He already knows about all kinds of weird stuff.

Abner looked at the floor, deep pain in his eyes. He gestured to her. "You might be magicals but you're dressed all strange-like and your accents sound odd." He nodded at Hana. "And you have a fox demon dame with a Japanese sword. If you have a Japanese magical helping you, I'm sure the war's long over."

"Dame?" Hana laughed. "You really are from the 1940s, aren't you?"

"And I don't even know what she is. Are you some kind of water nymph?" He pointed to Drysi's blue-streaked hair.

The witch laughed. "I'm fucking Welsh."

He harrumphed. "In my day, ladies didn't talk like that."

"Okay, Grandpa. I'm bloody Welsh and I dye my hair. Is that better?"

Hana smirked. "A nine-tailed fox isn't a demon, and even during World War II, you had Japanese-Americans serving in the US military doing all kinds of cool stuff like codebreaking."

The ensign shrugged. "No offense, Miss Sugimoto. I have nothing against anyone who had the stones to come to help this ship."

"You're right." Mason stepped forward. "It's been a while, and the war's long over. The Allies won decisively—including an unconditional surrender from the Japanese—but Japan, Germany, and the rest are all friends of the US now. That's not the biggest change, though."

"What is? Besides Welsh women who sound like some of the enlisted sailors."

Drysi snickered.

"The gates to Oriceran started to open a few decades back." The life wizard mimed a gate opening. "And now, magic's public knowledge on Earth. No one tries to hide it. The return of magic and the opening of gates caused trouble for a few years, but things aren't as bad as they could be. There are still wars, crime, and all that, but there has been no World War III, and most people are handling magicals living among them better than you'd expect."

Alison smiled at him, grateful that he'd given a quick synopsis without overwhelming the ensign. Over a century's worth of change had passed since the man set sail on the *Constantinople*, including social, economic, and historical upheaval. She couldn't imagine what it would be like to go through something like that. After all, she'd barely handled discovering a few secrets in her own life.

Abner stared at one of the engines, the worry etched deeply in his wrinkled forehead. "It's strange. I'm not surprised and it makes sense. This whole thing's been such a big snafu." He took a deep breath.

"If I might ask, Ensign Latherby—"

He shook his head. "Call me Abner. It seems silly to worry about my rank in this situation."

She gave him a grateful nod. "How long has it been for you?"

After a quick glance at his wristwatch, he shrugged. "A little over a day."

Drysi grimaced. "Does that mean that when we leave, decades will have passed? That's not what I wanted to hear."

Alison's heart rate kicked up. She'd always assumed they'd have until sunrise on Earth.

Damn it. It never even occurred to me that it might be a possibility.

"We don't know that." She infused confidence into her voice because she needed to set the example. "Even if it's true, there's nothing we can do about it. But it could be that the time dilation doesn't happen on this end until the ship disappears on Earth."

Abner frowned. "Disappears on Earth? You mean it's not still there? Isn't that why you came? We jumped and we finally came back? Then you came aboard to check, right?"

She shook her head. "I'm sorry, it's not like that at all. The ship appears between sundown on Halloween and sunrise the next day. It doesn't happen every year, but it's happened many times over the years."

The man scratched his cheek. "Every once in a while, the entire ship kind of fades away like it's turning into an actual ghost ship. The whole thing makes me want to lose my lunch—or it would if I'd eaten anything in a while. That must be what it is, the whole disappearing from Earth again."

Hana bit her lip. "Tahir might not wait for me if he has to wait decades." She tilted her head. "Then again, it is me." She patted her hip. "I'm worth it."

I'm glad someone can see the bright side.

"We experienced this weird reality distortion earlier," Alison explained. "All the colors changed, that kind of thing. Is that what you're talking about?"

Abner shook his head. "No, it's something different, Mrs. Brownstone. The strange part I'm talking about is like everything becomes less substantial and darker, with no colors really. Sound dies. Light dies. It lasts for several minutes."

"When was the last one?" Alison asked.

"About three hours ago. Sometimes, they happen closer together, but I haven't paid close attention to the pattern." He shrugged.

Mason glanced over his shoulder at the blue field. "A, if those fading events correspond to the teleports away from Earth, we still don't have any idea how to predict when the next one might be. We need to get out of here as soon as possible."

"Woah, slow your horses, cowboy." The ensign pointed to the shimmering crystal light show that floated in the air.

"We have to deal with that before we go anywhere. I couldn't do it alone, but now that I have you here, I can do what should have been done a day ago." His hands clenched into fists. "I told them all it was a bad idea but no one listened. Everyone was too worried about the Germans getting ahead. They said OSS found out that not only were German magicals doing things they shouldn't, but they might be getting help from nasty characters on Oriceran."

He shook his head. "Everyone knew how to say the right things to justify it. With the war going on, it was hard for guys like the Griffins to keep up." His lips curled into an angry frown. "It doesn't matter now. Good men are dead. They were good men who didn't want to do anything but defend their country and they don't even know why they died. Not only that, there's still a big threat."

Alison gestured toward the blue field. "Those monsters that tried to get in?"

Abner nodded. "This whole idea was supposed to be about jumping ships from one place to another without a detectable magical signature. I don't know where they obtained the artifacts for it, but they believed a big portal was too easy to detect—or it would be at the time, at least. I don't know about the world now that magic's everywhere. The problem is the jump didn't work on non-living things. The first thing they came up with was a jumping bomb, and that didn't work."

He scowled and drew a breath to continue. "They even admitted some were hurt in those first experiments. But they said if there was enough living energy to anchor the artifact, the whole process would work. Even though I was recruited to help in the ritual, I didn't understand much of it. All they told me was what I needed to know and no one shared much of the truth until after the jump. They told me for the magic to work, it couldn't be a small number of people and it couldn't be too many. They thought the *Constantinople*'s normal crew complement was exactly right, like a bowl of porridge for Goldilocks, but they weren't supposed to do this experiment. I know that now. I even knew it then, in the back of my head. It's why I made sure to go with them. I thought I could help if anything went wrong. But I couldn't do anything and I'm the only one left." He took another deep breath once he finished his explanation.

Alison's shoulders slumped. "You're the only one left?"

The man averted his eyes. "Most of them were killed right away. I'm sure you've seen it. They're somehow meshed with the ship. Then, the monsters came. People weren't even thinking about guns, not that it would have done them much good. We wizards were all clustered around the engine room in an attempt to find a solution. A few others left to gather survivors, but they never came back. The other guys who were with me left when they—" He took a few steps back and lowered his hand to his wand. "Why are you really here? You said it's been a long time and I put my first guess at twenty if not thirty years. Why now?"

"It's been a little over a hundred years." Alison raised her hands in front of her in a placating gesture. "We're here to help, Abner. Things are different in so many ways. Magic is out in the open now, but this little experiment isn't. You're right. They shouldn't have done it and they tried to bury it. For most of the country, the USS *Constantinople* never existed and the men on this ship died in different ways in the war."

"A hundred years? Then how did you find out?" he demanded, suspicion evident in both his voice and narrowed eyes.

"I will reach for something in my pocket," she explained, her voice soothing. She shook her head and gestured for her friends to keep their hands down. "It'll make everything clear if you see it."

"I want to believe you, Miss Brownstone." He kept his hand near the wand but didn't touch it.

She drew the music box slowly from a large vest pocket near her waist and held it in the palm of her hand.

The ensign's breath caught. He stared at it and his eyes watered. "It's been a day for me, but my Emmaline's long in her grave now. I gave that to her to remember me by and to always keep a connection." He uttered a pained laugh. "I didn't think it would help in this kind of situation. I thought I'd end up stranded on an island in the Pacific and she could give it to someone to trace me."

He's said a day twice now. That should have been enough time for something to happen with the bodies. I was right about time running differently, but Mason was also right about it being strange magic.

She nodded at the music box. "This was passed down through your family. It fell into the hands of your great-grandson. He hoped we could use it to save this ship and the sailors aboard, including you. If you're the only one left, that makes this easy. If we're right and time only passes when the ships fades, we can leave and you can meet him."

"Great-grandson?" Abner smiled. "It's not been a hundred years for me. It's been a day, but even in the last few hours, I wondered what—if we won the war and if anything had happened to Emmaline. The Latherby name lives on, huh?" He straightened his back and squared his shoulders. "I'd love to go and meet my great-grandson, but we can't. It's like I told you earlier. There's a big threat and as a member of the US Navy, I can't leave this ship until it's taken care of."

CHAPTER TWELVE

"By big threat do you mean those monsters?" Alison asked. "I can portal us out of here. We don't have to worry about them."

"I appreciate that, but we have to stabilize things first," Abner explained. "I didn't totally trust you until you showed me that music box. I wasn't sure if this was a Japanese trap or even someone from our side trying to cover up what they did. You've been square with me, so I'll be square with you. I know where those creatures are coming from. We discovered the answer. I think the others halfway knew already but it doesn't matter now. The important thing is that I know and I can tell you."

"I'm listening."

He pointed at the light inside the crystal formation. "It's a portal. Not to the World in Between—not from what we can tell and from what they told me. It's to somewhere else way stranger. That fog you've seen is kind of like the portal itself and bleeds over from that other world. Or maybe it is the other world. After all, it's not like they are hiding in the fog. They are the fog. One of us died learning that. It wasn't even that bad at first, only a little, then it was everywhere and it's only grown thicker."

"How many wizards were involved in this experiment?" she asked.

"There were six of us. One died during the initial jump. Two of us died trying to save the rest of the crew by bringing them here where we could protect them. It turns out crazy monsters can pick people off easy-like in narrow confines. There were three of us left after that. I was ordered to do everything I could to keep this artifact stable and protect it. When one of the creatures reached it, not only did it fade the ship, but it summoned even more of the fog and the artifact went crazy for a few minutes. Even if there were survivors, they were doomed after that."

The man shook his head at the memory. "The other wizard died trying to probe the artifact. He performed some kind of ritual I didn't recognize and told me all about the fog being partially like a portal and how we weren't simply seeing things and the fog itself was alive. He told me if I didn't keep the artifact stable, it might rip a bigger hole to that world. Then, he vaporized like he was an ice cube on the oven." He grimaced.

Drysi folded her arms and leaned against a nearby floor-to-ceiling pipe. "It sounds like this ritual involved magic that no one should have done, even if they were around today."

"That's what I believe," Abner admitted. "I should have done more to stop them, but I was an idiot and I thought they knew what they were doing."

"You said there were six wizards," Alison commented.

"But you only told me about four being dead. What happened to the other man?"

"Did you find a body in the enlisted mess?"

"The cafeteria-like place?" Alison asked. She nodded. "Yeah, there's a man we assumed was a wizard because he had a wand."

Abner furrowed his brow and put his hand to his chin. "He must still have them then."

"Have what?"

He coughed, the sound ragged. His hacking continued and he put his hand to his mouth and finally stopped after thirty seconds. Blood coated his palm.

Mason frowned and stepped toward him. "I can help you. I specialize in life magic."

The ensign put a hand up to stop him. "It's only magical strain. It takes so much to maintain the shields and do the spells needed to stabilize the crystals. Once we fix it, I'll be fine."

Hana wrinkled her nose. "There's an odd smell. It smells like…I don't know. Something magical but different than what we smelled before, but it's kind of familiar. And not in a good way."

"Fox dem—" He chuckled. "Nine-tailed foxes can smell magic? I didn't know that but I've never met one before either. I've only read about you."

He's hiding something and doesn't trust us totally, but after everything he's been through, I can't blame him.

"What do you think the dead wizard has?" Alison's tone was demanding. "You stopped before you finished explaining it."

"Amplification artifacts," he explained. "There are small

bronze coins inscribed with powerful sigils. They were originally supposed to be used to increase the range of the jump, but the guy you found explained that we could use them to shut this whole thing down and described what kind of spell we'd need. They had to be positioned in four particular locations on the ship. He needed me to stay here while he placed them. I used scrying when he didn't come back and found out what happened to him." He frowned. "I know what we need to do, but I would have had to drop the shields to shut everything down and that meant more monsters."

"Remember?" She shrugged. "I can portal us out of here. We'll bypass the monsters that way."

"No." Abner's tone turned strident. "We have to shut it down before we leave. I refuse to leave without doing that."

"You're not making yourself clear, Abner."

Drysi scoffed. "Who gives a shit about shutting it down? If you're the last man standing, we can take you and run."

"No," he snapped and gritted his teeth. "I'm coughing up blood because I needed more magic to keep everything stable. The only way I could think of to do that was to set up a ritual where I sacrificed my own lifeforce for magical power. It's not something I can maintain forever, but I can do it long enough to keep things under control until we fix things."

Alison inclined her head toward the witch. "She's right. If there aren't any survivors, we don't have to worry about this. We were willing to risk our lives to save sailors. I don't see the point of risking our lives to save the ship from monsters."

"That's not what this is about." He scrubbed a hand

down his face. "I know I haven't explained it all that well, but this is too dangerous to leave alone. If I don't stabilize it, everything will run out of control. The fog would grow greater, which means the portal to the other world will get bigger. Before, I simply tried to survive long enough for help to arrive, but you coming here makes it clear. A door swings both ways, Mrs Brownstone. I already failed my country and my fellow sailors by not stopping this experiment. I won't fail again by letting a horde of monsters pour out. I don't care if magic's out in the open. Most people don't have magic, and innocent people will get hurt." He pointed to a rank insignia on his shoulder. "I joined the Navy to protect my country, ma'am."

Hana pumped a fist in the air. "Hell, yeah. Let's close down the weirdo monster factory, Alison."

Drysi shrugged but her mouth quirked into a faint smile.

"If he's right, A," Mason began, "this could be a big problem. The *Constantinople* only appears in water, which means there might not be a rapid response from someone like an AET team. Who knows how many creatures could flood out before anyone discovers what's going on and takes action?"

Alison gave a firm nod. "I agree. Fine. Step one, stabilize the artifact to close the portal and stop the monsters. This will actually be easy. I can open a portal directly to the mess. We retrieve the coins and come here. I can then open a portal directly to each of the locations. Even if we have to fight the monsters, our exposure will be minimal."

"You can try, but someone already tried—the wizard in charge of this whole experiment." Abner pointed to the crystals. "This releases considerable magical interference. It doesn't seem to affect certain types of spells, but it wreaks havoc with portals and scrying. I could barely manage the spell I mentioned earlier."

"Yeah, but I'm…" She shrugged. "Let's say I'm special and leave it at that." She raised her hand and half-closed her eyes. Light and shadow poured into her efforts as she uttered the incantation and visualized her location. The magical strands dissipated as quickly as she could put them together. "Okay, not special enough in this case. You're right. There's too much interference."

"Where did you come in on the ship?" Abner asked.

"On the top, at the front and near a gun."

He looked thoughtful. "The foredeck. That makes sense. If you went far aft, it'd probably work, too, but it'd take less time to walk to the other place to place the coins than go there and open a portal. It's a gamble either way. If I take the field down, the monsters will swarm more. They feed off these artifacts somehow, and I can't let them get closer and make things less stable."

"You should stay here and maintain it then." Alison gestured to Mason. "He and I can set up two of the coins." She pointed to Drysi and Hana in turn. "They can do the others. We'll fight the monsters until you reset the field, then we'll go to the locations." She retrieved her phone and pulled up a blueprint of the ship class she'd downloaded at Ava's suggestion—and kicked herself mentally once again for not taking the time to study it earlier. "I don't know if this ship is laid out like others of its class, but if it is, we only need you to tell us where to go."

The ensign stepped forward and stared at the phone. "Is that some kind of artifact? I don't sense any magic."

"This is a phone. Well, a phone plus a computer."

He whistled. "You can carry your phones. And a computer? What's that? Is it like a miniature movie theater?"

She waved a hand to stop the questions. "Don't worry about it. We only need you to show us where to go."

Abner took the phone gingerly and squinted at the small blueprint. He jabbed his finger in four different places. "Near the forward gun would work. You know where that is. Boatswain's stores, also in the front of the ship, but a few decks down. Aft storeroom, and aft berthing."

"Of course, we would have to go as far away as possible," Drysi griped. "Why can't saving the world ever be easy?"

"Once you have them placed, I can do the final spell and that should shut everything down, but I don't have any way to talk to you if I'm here. The scrying spell only worked because what I looked at was so close, and it almost didn't. I can hear things and people right outside the shield, but that's it."

She absorbed that information, worried for a moment, then smiled. "It's fine. We can communicate with each other using walkie-talkie mode on our phones, and we can loan you one." She nodded to Hana. "Get yours out. Let's see if it works."

The fox complied. She swiped and tapped a few times. "Ready?"

Alison activated her walkie-talkie mode. "Test, test, test."

The other woman held her phone to her ear and shook her head, her lips pursed in irritation.

"So there's too much electromagnetic interference, too?" The Drow frowned. "Damn. Okay. We'll do this the old-fashioned way. We'll retrieve the coins from the mess and split up. Drysi and Hana will take the aft rooms and Mason and I will take the bow rooms. Once a team is finished, they should head to the engine room. Then, we shut this thing down and take Abner home."

"That simple, huh?" Drysi grinned.

"As simple as fighting through strange monsters to set up artifacts in particular places for a complicated ritual that may or may not work."

Hana patted her hilt. "We've been in worse situations before. That's what we do, kick ass and save the world."

The witch laughed. "We've fought nastier bastards, for sure, but I don't think we've been trapped halfway to another dimension while doing it."

Mason smirked at Alison. "Did you decide that now we're married, we have to up the challenges to keep things fresh?"

She shrugged. "I need to keep up with Dad. Let's hurry. We can't know for sure how long we can stay before we're stuck. Let's do this as quickly as possible and get the hell out of here." She turned to Abner. "Are you ready?"

He lifted his wand. "Keep them off me and I'll throw up a new shield. Since I won't be able to say it later, good luck and Godspeed."

CHAPTER THIRTEEN

The Brownstone team spent a couple of minutes preparing for combat before Abner dropped the shield. None of the earlier monsters haunted the front of the engine room or the passage, but the corridor that led to the mess was choked by the fog, which no longer seemed afraid. They took a few steps forward while the ensign continued to cast his spell.

It didn't take long for the fog to coalesce into new creatures, many the same types as before, including the previously invulnerable specters. A new one joined them this time, a bright yellow crablike creature with two rows of seven eyes. It was almost cute in a strange cartoony way.

Alison pointed to one. "Wait for him and slice with the *tachi*, Hana."

The fox saluted and stepped out of the line of fire. Alison, Mason, and Drysi launched a torrent of death through the narrow space, including a stream of shadow crescents and Drysi's piercing beam, while Mason alternated between ice blasts and bright arrows of light magic.

The pentapods and worms fell after only a few attacks. The specters continued their advance and the spells passed through them with no apparent effect. It took several combined attacks to crack the shells of the crabs and several more to shear limbs and parts from their bodies before they succumbed and faded into thick gray smoke. The pentapods were easy to kill but took the longest to vanish, although it didn't take as long as it had before.

Every monster that formed reduced the amount of fog, and as that declined, fewer creatures appeared. The smoke from the dead obscured some of the new arrivals, but even that dissipated quickly under the continual assault from the Brownstone team. Alison maintained her shadow crescent assaults and sweat beaded on her forehead. She didn't always appreciate that things could prove more challenging when she couldn't overwhelm her enemy with one massive barrage. It took considerable effort to keep up a rapid stream of attacks.

One of the specters entered the engine room and plodded toward the Drow. Hana ducked low and sliced through it with the *Tachi*. The two portions of its faint body slid apart before they melted into the residual smoke in the room.

"Ha!" The fox leapt aside. "Maybe I should call my sword Ghostkiller. Or Ghostkilla."

Alison bisected another pentapod. "I don't think they're technically ghosts and I don't think you should name the sword."

"Whatever." The woman took advantage of a quick lull in spells to sprint across the front of the room to attack the other specters, her movement almost a blinding blur with her bright tails waving behind her. Once the path ahead was clear, her teammates restarted their own assault.

I take it for granted how calm everyone is in this kind of situation. This shit's extreme, even by Dad's standard, and no one blinks.

Abner's containment field glowed into being behind them. The existing monsters didn't stop or disappear and forced the Brownstone team to continue the battle until the only things left in the passage were the twitching remains of pentapods that sublimated slowly into the gray smoke.

The Drow took ragged breaths. "That was annoying, but I don't see any fog. I hope we can find the coins without much trouble." She didn't bother to conjure a shadow blade. There wasn't enough room for her to swing it if she wanted the rest of the team to be able to attack. That aside, she didn't feel the need to develop a signature fighting style for adventures on Naval vessels. She doubted it would be a huge part of her career.

They hurried to the enlisted mess, which was mercifully fog-free.

Finally, some luck.

"Maybe we won't have any more trouble," Hana commented and looked around, her sword still in her hand. "The fog avoided us before. Now that we kicked its ass again, it'll be scared."

"That would be nice." Alison knelt beside the slain wizard. "I doubt we'll be that lucky, but we know we can beat them." She took a deep breath and reached into the man's pockets. Her fingers found a stack of something cold and round and she withdrew the coins.

She turned them over and examined them. They were thick and about an inch in diameter. Identical intricate arcane symbols had been etched deeply into both sides of each one and faint magic radiated off them.

"Abner didn't say anything about a particular coin needing to be in a particular place." She held two out to Drysi, who took them and passed them to Hana.

The Welsh witch scowled. "And what if he forgot?"

"Then we'll find out the hard way." She tucked the remaining two in her pocket. "If you encounter trouble, head to the engine room. If necessary, we can tackle it with the full group."

Hana sheathed her sword. "We can do this fine, don't worry. You do what you need to do and we'll do the same."

"I won't die here, Alison," Drysi declared. "I'll never let myself die in a place like this." She pointed her thumb over her shoulder at the other woman. "She's not even a witch. I'd embarrass myself if I let her outperform me."

"You know you love me, Drysi," the fox taunted.

Alison looked at Mason. "Time for a little date."

I like being strong like Alison, Hana thought, *but I hate when it involves gross monsters.*

She growled and sliced through two pentapods before she bounded toward a crystalline worm and raised her blade. Drysi blasted spells to annihilate several more enemies. Their trip to the first target room had been uneventful. With each step, the fog had retreated, but once they arrived at their destination, it surged forward and coalesced into another horde of creatures eager to murder them.

"It's like they know what we're doing," the fox shouted. A pentapod swung at her and she jumped aside, not wanting to test her artifact against the strange adversaries. "Like it's a defense mechanism."

The witch whipped her wand up and shouted a spell. The door slammed shut and the handle spun itself until it clicked closed.

Hana grinned and flourished her blade. "How do you like that, fog freaks? You can't go through—"

Loud pounding came from the door.

Drysi took a deep breath and held her wand pointed at it. "We still have to go out that way. Get the coin into position and we can move on."

The pounding grew louder, as did the sound of wrenching metal.

Hana fished one out of her pocket. She strode to a crate near the back and set the coin on top of it. With her blade in her right hand, she retrieved her gun with her left. "You might as well open—"

A pentapod blade erupted through the metal like the alien monster had made its best attempt to audition for *The Shining.*

"Oh, come on!" the fox shouted. "That's not fair. It's a metal door."

After a few more slices, a charge by a yellow crab drove the entire door to the floor and the loud crash reverberated through the narrow passage. She opened fire and emptied her magazine. The volley sent several pentapods and worms to the land of smoke before she dropped her gun and hacked through a specter.

Drysi conjured another purple death beam. Hana didn't want to ask her about it. She'd not seen the spell used before, which suggested it might be darker magic. The witch circled toward the corner of the room to give her teammate more room to swing her blade.

"I hope Alison has an easier time because this is annoying." The fox swung her sword to cut through one of the four-legged shadows. Despite its insubstantial nature, she felt more resistance cutting through the shadow monsters than she did with the pentapods. "And there are so many of them."

Drysi grimaced in pain and her eyes were bloodshot. She carved through several adversaries with another purple beam. The enemy force had diminished and the fog had thinned somewhat. The Brownstone team was winning, but they had to put up a major fight to do so.

"Are you okay?" Hana spun to avoid an attack by a pentapod blade. If it cut through solid metal, it might realistically carve through her ring-activated defensive shield. A serious injury would delay them too long, and it didn't matter if she was healed if she ended up trapped in time for a few decades.

"I'm all right but I won't lie, this spell takes a hell of a lot out of me." The witch hissed and thrust her wand out. The purple beam scythed through six different enemies to destroy the bulk of those still ranged against them.

"Rest, Drysi." The other woman surged forward. "I'll get this." She twirled and spun while her blade flashed rhythmically until not a single adversary remained. What little fog was left retreated down the passage. "Uh-huh. I thought so. That's what you get for screwing with Sword Fox and Blue Witch."

Drysi eyed her dubiously. "Sword Fox and Blue Witch?"

"You don't feel it? Either of them?"

Her companion shook her head.

"Oh, well." Hana walked backward, her sword still up while she watched the fog until she reached her gun. She sheathed her blade, reloaded the weapon, and slid it into a holster. "New rule—stay away from boats. They're always annoying."

The Welsh witch took a few deep breaths. "Damn. I feel like shit."

"Why have you used that spell?"

"It's difficult to explain if you don't know magic. It can hurt things that normally can't be hurt." She tucked her wand away and pulled an energy potion out of a pouch, downed the contents, and tossed the empty vial on the floor. "This might not be the World in Between, but I wanted to be sure. I think I'll have to hold off on using it again, though. It fucks me up, and it's technically a type of curse. I'm not sure Alison will like that once she realizes it, even if it does lead to a tidy fight against these fog monsters."

The other woman nodded slowly and sighed. "I don't think Alison would care that much about curses, but I do think she cares about you damaging yourself in the fight. If she gives you any heat, I'll bust her for being a hypocrite." She rolled her eyes. "That girl walked around trying to save the world when she was still infected with that stupid anti-magic virus. She's the poster girl for trying too hard."

Drysi snorted. "And she was still dangerous. I'm decent

with a gun and in a fight, but if my magic was weak, I'd be nothing. I wouldn't last a minute in a battle against any halfway skilled magical."

"I have the claws, the speed, and the body," Hana mused, "but the sword and the ring help. Like you always say, I won't lie." She snickered. "I can't say I ever imagined in my entire life that I would end up in a place like this." She walked into the passage. "According to the blueprint, we need to take the ladder up and head to the final room."

The witch trailed after her. "I don't know what I thought about my life. For the longest time, I believed I'd die at the hands of someone the Seventh Order wanted me to kill. It's not like I wanted to die, but when you're an assassin, you know you could at any moment. It seems kind of poetic that way. When I met Alison..." She frowned. "In the beginning, I wished she wasn't so damned concerned about helping people. It would have made having to kill her so much easier."

Hana shrugged and sniffed the air. Residual magic still lingered but the nauseatingly sweet scent she associated with the fog was much weaker than before.

"If she hadn't been concerned with helping you, you might have ended up dead." She patted her chest over her heart. "I'm at peace with my former scumbag ways. It's nice having a best friend who gave me a well-paying job that led to me a relationship with a hot, cute, and smart guy." She wiggled her hips and the motion shook the sheath. "And the toys are fun, too."

"Do you ever miss it?" Drysi asked.

"Conning people?"

Her companion nodded. "I don't miss assassinating

people, but there was a certain challenge to the hunt. Working with Alison almost makes it too easy."

The fox tapped her bottom lip. "You know what? I really don't. I used to. It was the same kind of thing I enjoyed—the challenge. I loved it when I could win without having to resort to my fox charm but now, it feels...wrong, you know? Every once in a while, we need my charm for the job and I don't mind it, but I feel happier being on Team Hero than Team Criminal."

Drysi uttered a dark chuckle. "I can't compare us. You stole people's money. I killed them. I won't lie, many of them were right bastards anyway who deserved to die, but I can't say that's true of all of them. I didn't know anything about most of them. I was given a job and I did it, all to help the Seventh Order and their twisted plans."

Hana ran her hands along the cool metal surface of the bulkheads. It might be warm above deck, but the deeper they traveled into the ship, the chillier it became. "I suppose our lives are much like this ship."

"What?" Drysi's face scrunched in confusion.

"It's kind of convoluted, but think about it." Hana arrived at the ladder, caught hold of a rung, but didn't climb. "There are so many weird secrets out there. I'm a fox and you're a witch. We would have been secrets in the past. Even with the gates open, magic's still a big deal. Between Tapestry, Omni, and the creatures on this ship, it's not like we have a clue about all the possible varieties of monsters that might be out there, lurking in the shadows in another dimension or on an alien planet. Even the truth about magic was always there, waiting to be revealed when the time was right."

The woman nodded slowly but her expression suggested she thought she had gone crazy. She didn't mind because she often looked at her like that.

"The truth wasn't out because, for thousands of years, no one wanted the truth to be known," the witch explained. "It was a conspiracy."

"I know. But think about what things could have been like if people had known. Sure, the gates weren't open yet, but we still had access to magic. The world could have been a different place—a better place."

Drysi shrugged. "What's the point of worrying about the past? You can't change it. The only thing you can do is make sure you don't make the same mistakes in the future."

Hana grinned and tapped the side of her head. "And that's why we're like this boat."

The other woman laughed. "Sometimes, I let the whole happy fox thing trick me. You were a con artist. You have so much going on in that fashion- and Tahir-obsessed brain of yours."

"Stupid con artists don't last long." The fox climbed to a higher rung.

CHAPTER FOURTEEN

Alison pulled herself through the open hatch and onto the deck with a loud grunt. Hopefully, Drysi and Hana were close to finishing the placement of their coins. She understood the threat the ship posed but she also wondered if they'd be trapped in time like Abner.

At least my husband's with me so he doesn't have to wonder what happened.

She and Mason had already battled through another horde of monsters to set up a coin in the boatswain's stores. After one last coin deposit near the forward gun, they could hurry to the engine room, do what had to be done, and get everyone back to Earth.

The monsters are annoying but we carve through them fairly well and they know to leave us alone after a fight. In a way, we've been as lucky as the crew of this ship was unlucky.

They had been too late to save the sailors, but at least they could get one man back to Earth and provide closure for the Latherby family. Stopping a potential threat was a nice bonus.

Although enemies had opposed them on the way to the location for the first coin—including a strange floating eyeball with sharp spines—the fog remained in full retreat. A few yards out from the forward gun, it remained thick and provided an obscuring albeit shifting wall, but it didn't form into any new attackers. She had many questions about its true nature, but she was content to let the mystery linger in her mind if it meant they could escape.

An odd sensation passed through her. It felt almost like magic, but there was something off about the sensation. It made the hair on the back of her neck stand up.

It is still Halloween. We might run into actual spirits, too.

"Did you feel that?" she asked and looked around.

Mason frowned. He pulled his wand out and cast another shield spell on himself. "The monsters might have decided they're tired of letting us kick their asses. Or they're hungry."

Alison raised her hand and summoned her own shield. She took a deep breath, conjured a blade, and extended shadow wings. Now that she wasn't trapped in a cramped space below deck or a narrow passage, she could fight using her preferred style. She didn't care if it was monsters or ghosts and simply didn't have time to mess around in a fight.

A noise ripped through the quiet night. She didn't want to believe what she was hearing because it was so unexpected. Her brain almost couldn't comprehend the crazy reality. A few more seconds passed and she couldn't deny the truth. Someone was slow-clapping.

"What now?" she muttered and stared into the fog

toward the source of the sound. "Clap demons here to mock us before they try to kill us?"

Four dark humanoid forms appeared. She raised her blade and the figures advanced until their features resolved into Drow in armor. Immediately, she recognized the tall man in the middle of the group. A thin necklace of bright green twined hair rested around his neck. Now that he was closer, she could tell it was the source of the strange magic she'd felt earlier.

"Marat?" She scowled. "What the hell are you doing here? I don't know how you got here, but this is not a place you want to be. I don't have time to explain."

The Drow all raised their arms and summoned shadow blades.

Damn it. So much for being lucky.

A wicked smile crossed the man's face. He motioned to the necklace. "My princess has been very generous to me. In return, she asks certain tasks of me. I didn't anticipate that I would have to—" He frowned. "Where are we?"

Alison shrugged. "That's a good question. But I don't understand. What does this have to do with Novati? If you want me to apologize for what happened, I won't. She's the one who challenged me. You're the one who issued the damned challenge on her behalf. Now, we need to finish a ritual and get the hell off this ship before we are all trapped in time."

"I don't care what you have to say." Marat shook his head. "And you don't understand, Princess Alison. Novati isn't my princess. Princess Drae is and has been for some time. She has given me an important task that I must carry out."

She narrowed her eyes. "That answers a few questions I had about what happened on Oriceran. You're a damned traitor."

"No, I'm not a traitor. My loyalty is what it has always been—to the Drow people. Princess Drae has plans that will help lead us into the future. That won't be possible if we allow a half-human on the throne." His nostrils flared. "Your father weakened us and you would destroy us, but I'll destroy you first."

"Me?" She pointed to herself. "I'm the one who will destroy the Drow? Laena's arrogance was responsible for her problems. She had many opportunities to leave me alone and leave my father alone, but she couldn't stop. It was Drae, not me, who tried to murder a number of other Drow with a backhanded, sleazy scheme. Every time I've tried to step away, a Drow has targeted me and finally, Rasila's begun to make far more sense."

The Drow sneered. "For all your magical strength, your spirit is weak and far too human. That is all the more reason for you to die." He tilted his chin, dismissive disdain written in his face. "My princess does offer you one last chance to agree to a binding ritual. We can perform it here. You don't have to die in this place."

Mason snorted. "Do you really think she'll agree to that?"

"Silence, human. Your thoughts on this aren't our concern, but don't think you won't die if we kill her."

Alison inclined her head toward Mason. "He's right, you know. If I didn't agree to this crap before Drae tried to kill me and murdered my friend, why would I do it now?"

"Because you don't want to be queen of the Drow," he

shouted. "You've said this to many of us in the past yet you continue to interfere."

She rolled her eyes scornfully. "I tried to keep out of things but you assholes couldn't leave me alone so, yeah, my attitude's changed. You're right. My father did play a role in creating this mess, and I'll play a role in stopping it. And I'll guarantee you something. There's no way in hell I'll let Drae become queen, even if that means I have to do something ridiculous like put Omni on the throne. Understood?"

His eyebrows raised. "Who is Omni?"

Mason smirked. "Does that make me a king?"

"No, sorry. The way Drow rules work, you'll technically be my consort." She offered him an apologetic smile.

He laughed. "Mason Lind, Royal Consort. I could live with that. It's a nice gig."

"Silence!" Marat thundered. "Do you think this is a joke?"

"No," she replied. "But I think you're a joke. You should turn and leave while you still have a chance. Normally, I wouldn't care, but like I said, I'm in the middle of some-thing here so I'd rather not waste time with you assholes begging to die." She narrowed her eyes. "And do you honestly think you have any chance to win against me? You might not like me, but that doesn't change the fact I'm Drow royalty who has beaten other Drow royals."

"Yes, you are." He ran this finger over the necklace. Purple-black shadows oozed from the accessory and covered his neck. "You're right, Princess of the Shadow Forged. I would have lacked the power to follow or track you before but with this, I will kill you and your human husband. I will protect my people." Inky blackness covered his eyes. "And I will serve my princess and the Drow. You were given your one chance to surrender. Now, you'll die."

Mason tucked his wand into his holster and cracked his knuckles. "You're damned arrogant."

The Drow bared his teeth. "Don't worry, wizard. You'll be dead before Princess Alison. Then, we can destroy her father who humiliated our people."

Alison barked out a laugh. "You plan to attack my dad? You're even stupider than I thought."

"He will be weak with grief." Marat cut through the air with his hand. "He'll be easy to defeat."

"Let me tell you a little story. When I first met him—before he adopted me obviously—he had a pet. That dog was the only thing he cared about in the world. Some gangsters thought like you do—that they could weaken him by killing what he loved—so they killed it." She glowered. "He was sad but he also got very, very mad. When everything was over, it wasn't only the gangsters who killed his dog who were dead. Their entire organization had been wiped off the face of the planet." She bent her knees and shunted shadow magic into her legs.

Her adversary and his allies spread out, their attention almost completely focused on her.

She scoffed. "Assuming you managed to kill me, this wouldn't end with you killing my dad. It would probably end with my dad going full Vax." She summoned another blade but continued to channel magic into her legs. "So, here's the thing. I have to kill you now, not because you've threatened me and not even because you work for a duplicitous, murderous bitch who set my friend up to die. I have to kill you to make sure this plot ends here and it doesn't end with Oriceran being destroyed."

"I will enjoy killing you, Alison Brownstone." Marat spat on the deck. "You are no princess of the Drow. You're nothing but a human in the end."

"Who knows? Fairly soon, I might be queen." Alison released the energy and launched toward the enemy. Mason burst into a near blur. She arrived in seconds and swung the blade in her left hand at one of the Drow. He stumbled and his shield weakened. She stabbed at Marat. He parried her blade, but the force of her attack pushed him back. Before he could retaliate, she elevated quickly.

Mason closed the gap and barreled into another of the assassins. He battered relentlessly and his enhanced punches strained his opponent's shield and edged him closer to the destroyer's railing.

The only adversary who hadn't been attacked flung dark orbs at Alison. A few pounded into her shield and stung but didn't make it through. She rotated and dive-bombed Marat while she fired small explosive shadow bullets at him. The Drow assassin hissed as her attack penetrated his shield and shredded his chest.

Shadow grew immediately from the edges of the wound and he raised his arm. A humming orb, a deep purple-black color, erupted from his palm into the sky and narrowly missed her. It detonated into a shadow of wriggling, shadowy tentacles that squirmed toward her and exploded on touch. The other Drow filled the air with a near-constant stream of attacks.

Mason continued to hammer at his opponent and gave him no rest. The man tried to stab him, but he sidestepped and caught his arm. He bent it back and the Drow cried out in pain when his bones snapped. The life wizard didn't cease his attack. He continued to shove his arm back, limb and shadow blade together, until it reached the man's neck. It sliced halfway through before the blade faded and a roundhouse kick did the rest. It was hard to heal or regenerate without a head.

Alison dodged and looped to avoid the constant stream of attacks that assailed her. Marat laughed as he launched another wriggler bomb. Several tentacles exploded against her shield and this time, punched through. She gritted her teeth and forced the sharp pain of her burns out of her mind. She dove directly toward one of the other Drow and strafed him with shadow bullets. He raised his arm to reinforce his depleted shield, but the momentary lapse was enough for her to connect and slice through him with her blades. He groaned and coughed up blood. She launched herself up again and brought her blades down in the middle to carve him into three pieces.

These guys don't know when to give up.

Marat's eyes widened and he staggered away as he channeled shadow magic into a growing, shuddering mass of darkness. His remaining ally tried to charge her but a massive fireball erupted around him.

Her gaze slid to the side. Mason stood a few yards away and grinned, his fingers loose around his wand. She nodded to her husband and took to the sky again to circle Marat and shower him with shadow crescents. The attacks missed, sliced into the deck metal, and dug deep holes.

The life wizard rushed toward the other assassin while he delivered another couple of fireballs. It wasn't enough to kill the man, but it was enough to deplete his defenses. Mason tossed his wand into his left hand and brought his fist back. He drove it into the Drow's face with a loud crunch, and his opponent catapulted away and cracked his head against the hard metal of the huge turret. He slumped, his neck at an unnatural angle.

"Definitely not royalty," the wizard muttered. He spun toward Marat and launched a fireball.

The Drow growled as a fireball and shadow crescent struck him at the same time. He jerked and released his spell. The dark sphere hurtled toward Alison, but she dodged it with ease. It continued its flight and disappeared into the fog. A second later, a bright purple flash lit up the area and the entire boat shook. The sound of wrenching metal was followed by another loud crash that made the vessel shudder alarmingly.

Yeah, that didn't sound good. The bastard will sink this boat or worse if we don't kill him.

Alison zigzagged over her enemy. For all his newfound power, he very pointedly made no effort to fly. She didn't attack and left it to Mason to pelt the Drow from a distance with fireballs and ice lances. While he distracted their enemy, she continued to feed magic into her sword. It grew inch by inch and darkened with its new size. The mild light of the fog, night, and her light orb were swallowed and the blade looked more like a hole in the night than a weapon.

"You will never be queen, Alison Brownstone!" Marat screamed. "You don't deserve it."

She skimmed the deck, released her wings, and rolled upright into a sprint. "Maybe, but you'll not be around to worry about it." She swung her blade. It sliced into him, and a wave of purple-tinged black blasted from the impact site to launch pieces of him over the railing.

His remains pitched into the ocean below and landed with an audible splash.

Relieved, she released her spell and took a deep breath. Emerald lightning blasted through the fog all around them.

"That can't be good."

Mason jogged to her. "Set the coin down and let's get back to Abner before we're stuck here and need someone to rescue us."

CHAPTER FIFTEEN

When Alison and Mason raced to the engine room, they found Drysi and Hana waiting for them. Abner didn't want to lower the shield until he was ready but once she described the lightning, he dropped it immediately. To everyone's surprise, no new monsters arrived. It was then that she realized something she hadn't noticed on the way back to the engine room.

"There wasn't any fog inside the ship," she explained. "Not fog that retreated—no fog at all, but it's way thicker up top, not to mention the lightning."

The ensign smiled. "Good."

"That's good?"

"Not the lightning, but the rest makes things easier." He raised his wand. "The amplifiers are in place and your efforts seem to have scared off the monsters based on what you said. I can do what I need to do and deactivate the artifact. If all goes well, it should close the portal and return the *Constantinople* to Earth. I'm only sorry it took so long."

He pointed to the door. "You need to get back above deck so you can portal to Earth."

She shrugged. "What's the point? You'll bring the ship back, right? We'll travel with you."

He shook his head. "The only thing I'm confident about is that I can seal the portal. There's a good chance the ship will come back too, but I can't be sure of that. And if it does come back, it'll go through the same magic as it did the first time. I can't be sure that you won't be sealed in a bulkhead. I didn't trust the magic then and I trust it even less now."

Hana frowned. "What about you? Can't you set it on automatic or something? You might end up all...you know, inside something."

"No, I can't set it on automatic and it doesn't matter anyway." His shoulders and head slumped.

"You can't give up now, Grandpa," Drysi insisted.

"Grandpa?" Abner uttered a quiet chuckle. "You look older than me."

"You're over a hundred." The witch grinned. "And you're a military man. You have to keep fighting until you're dead. "You survived when no one else did. You can't give up now."

"That's just it, I already am."

She shook her head. "Fighting doesn't mean only stopping the monsters. It also means surviving."

The ensign's chuckle sounded pained. "You don't understand. I'm already dead."

Hana gasped. Alison stared at him, her mouth agape in disbelief. She'd run into any number of weird things in her life but somehow, the world constantly managed to surprise her.

Mason pulled his wand out and murmured a spell. "What the hell?"

Hana sniffed the air. "Oh, shit. That's what it smells like. It kind of reminds me of what those Tapestry assholes smelled like and they borrowed dead bodies for their work." She winced. "No offense, Abner."

"None taken. I don't know what the Tapestry is, but you're right. I'm currently an abomination and I think, under normal circumstances, the spell wouldn't have even worked. I'm disgusted with myself, but it was necessary."

Alison stared at him. "No normal spell can bring someone back to life. Maybe a wish, but I doubt you had access to one unless you're far more special than we realized."

"There was no wish, only my magic, and it didn't bring me back to life. It merely delayed my death for a little longer. I couldn't die, not until I knew people would be safe. Someone might be able to say that I'm more between life and death than truly dead."

"You're a zombie?"

Drysi raised a hand. "I think he's more a lich."

"Wow." Hana's face filled with admiration. "You're something else, Abner. You don't stop even when you're dead. Respect."

"I never thought I'd be praised by a fox demon." The man fumbled in his pocket and withdrew a small silver locket. He opened it and turned it to show everyone. It contained a black-and-white picture of a pretty dark-haired young woman in a high-necked dress.

"My Emmaline," he explained and snapped it shut. "I know she's long since met her maker, but I don't want this picture of her to die with me. I want it to be with my family." He pulled a pocket watch out. "This is an heirloom. It was supposed to be a good luck charm." He held his watch arm up. "I don't even keep it wound since I have this. The pocket watch was intended as a gift for my son when he turned eighteen, but it can be a gift to my great-grandson." He offered both to the Drow. "Please. There's no other way."

She accepted them with a sigh. Hana turned away, her eyes glistening as the reality of the situation finally settled in.

"Now, go," Abner insisted. "I don't know what that lightning means, but you're right. That part can't be a good sign. I need to finish this and you need to get out of here."

Mason squeezed Alison's shoulder. "Let's go, A. Don't make his sacrifice in vain."

She took a deep breath and released it slowly. "I'm sorry we couldn't get here sooner, Abner."

"Don't be sorry, Mrs Brownstone," he replied. "I couldn't have positioned the coins without you so you arrived exactly when you were needed. Despite everything that has happened, I consider that kind of lucky."

"Then you have a much better attitude toward life than I do."

———

Their lifeboat bobbed on the mild ocean waves. Alison had suggested they take one because she wanted to see if the experiment worked from a reasonably close distance. Her portal magic, in combination with the music box's links to Earth, allowed them to exit the strange magical pocket with far greater ease than they had entered. Now, they floated fifty yards from the *Constantinople* in an ancient lifeboat, waiting for a dead man to complete his final mission.

Honor and duty, huh?

She could see why people had difficulty making out any details in the earlier sightings. From outside, the fog and magical field covered the whole ship, bent the light inside, and obscured any distinctive attributes. Would knowing it was the *Constantinople* have helped? She couldn't help but wonder. If wizards had stormed the ship in the forties or fifties, maybe the sailors who had survived the jump might have been saved.

"It's still a win, A," Mason reminded her softly. A good husband could always read a wife's mind from her expression alone. "If Abner was the only one keeping those monsters under control, it wouldn't have been long before he...couldn't manage it anymore. The next thing you know, Canada would be invaded by a monster army pouring from another dimension. An entire night is a long time for a monster horde to grow."

"I know." She managed a weak smile. "And I defeated Marat and made Drae waste a powerful artifact. It's a few victories for Team Brownstone."

Hana rolled her eyes. "I can't believe he tried to kill you on the ship of all places. What a putz."

"Even he was a little surprised, but that means we might be busy soon. If Drae tried to assassinate me, it also means she's ready to make her move. She has to know I'll go directly to Rasila."

The fox sighed. "There is no rest for the wickedly sexy."

A column of blinding yellow light bathed the ship and rocketed into the sky. Hana gasped and covered her mouth with her hand.

Drysi squinted. "I think that means it worked. Or it could mean we're all about to die."

Alison nodded slowly and forced herself to look at the bright light. The column persisted for about thirty seconds before it vanished. The *Constantinople* reappeared, this time without the fog or the magic field.

Hana bolted to her feet with a cheer and rocked the boat.

The witch glared at her. "Remember what this means."

"Sorry," she said sheepishly and sat carefully.

They waited in respectful silence for a couple of minutes. The fox's eyes widened and she pointed. Abner's white-clad form walked toward the railing and waved before he stepped away toward the turret.

"I'll be right back," Alison said. She grew shadow wings, flew toward the ship, and landed near the turret and the ensign. "You did it."

"My only regret is that I couldn't do more."

"I think everyone who tries to make the world a better place feels that way. The world isn't perfect, but we did win the war and beat the fascists. Emmaline lived in a time of relative peace and prosperity, and your child grew up to have children."

"Thank you for telling me that. And thank you for being here, but my time is over. Without the artifact active,

I don't have enough magical power left to maintain what I've been doing. I hope I've done my great-grandson proud." He smiled.

She nodded. "You have, Abner. You have. You've done him and your country proud."

Smiling, he crumbled into dust and left only his uniform.

"Good job, sailor." She wiped a tear away. "You did your duty to the end and protected your country and even your planet." She suddenly realized something, felt in her pocket, and pulled her receiver out. Quickly, she inserted into her ear and tapped it. "Tahir, please tell me you can hear me. Are you okay?"

"I'm fine. Why wouldn't I be?" he asked.

"Drow assassins crashed the party," she replied wearily.

"How is that even possible?" he asked and almost sounded shocked.

"With help from a powerful artifact, from what I can tell. Don't worry. I killed them."

"What happened?" he replied. "Did you bounce out of the ship because of the Drow attack? I'm surprised you defeated them so quickly."

Alison frowned in confusion. "I don't follow you."

"You entered the portal and I lost contact with you, but then you came out of that portal in the lifeboat a minute later and the whole ship returned. I still had interference but it cleared up when you contacted me."

"It's a long story." She sighed. "But I'll give you the short version because I need you to send a little something to a reporter."

"A reporter?" The infomancer's voice filled with skepticism.

"Jenna Jordan. I'll give her a big scoop and if she acts quickly, she can be out in front of this. I don't want anyone in the government to bury it because they think their secrets should stay hidden. Contact her immediately once I give you the details. Get her on the phone. I know you can do it and keep it anonymous."

"Ah. I'm glad I'll be able to contribute, then. And...Hana is fine? I don't have a good angle with any satellites at the moment."

She glanced at the lifeboat in the distance. "Yeah, she's fine. I promise I won't pull a stunt like this for a while."

CHAPTER SIXTEEN

A little desperate, Alison snuggled under her blanket and turned on her side. The softness of her bed and the warm presence of her husband did little to quell her tumultuous thoughts and her mind simply wouldn't shut off. The exhaustion was overwhelming, and she was close to using a spell or potion to get some rest.

Mason stirred beside her and yawned. "We had a rough night, A. You should really get some sleep. I told you before. It was a win. There's nothing we could have done other than what we did. Without us, the ship would have stayed a monster factory forever."

"He did his duty to the end," she murmured half into her pillow. "Shit. Beyond the end. Think about how crazy that is."

"That's what it means to be in the military. I don't mean to be dismissive, but he understood the risks when he joined."

She sat up quickly. "Marat thought he was doing his duty, too, but he also thought he would win. I don't think he walked into that fight thinking it was suicide. But it has made me think about duty."

He stared at her, his head still on the pillow. "A, you know I love and respect you, right?"

"You married me, so I would hope so. But why do you say that?"

"If this is about the Drow, I'll back you, no matter what choice you make. If this is about becoming queen, I'll back you in that, too."

Alison managed a smile. "You only want to be a royal consort."

Mason rolled onto his back and closed his eyes. "Hey, there are worse things than being able to brag about sleeping with a queen." He grinned.

Despite being at Maneki, she didn't feel like it was victory sushi. That was also why she didn't invite any of her friends.

Agent Latherby knelt in front of a low table across from her, stone-faced. They were in a private back room and both magicals had taken measures to protect themselves from eavesdropping, both magical and mundane.

A few days had passed since Halloween. Alison had already told him the details of what had happened over a secure call, with the exception of Marat's visit. It wasn't relevant to the agent's personal mission, and she didn't want the government up her ass about Drow matters. No matter what she decided, she wanted it to be without unnecessary outside pressure. When she had checked with

Rasila, the other princess revealed that she'd lost a few spies in recent weeks, but there had been no direct attacks or assassination attempts on her. She told her to stand by and wait for her to contact her. For today, she would worry about her meeting with Latherby and giving his family closure.

She picked up a piece of salmon nigiri and plopped it into her mouth, chewed and savored the flavor, and swallowed. Even if the mood wasn't jubilant, the sushi was still damned good.

"So, here we are," she said quietly. "I'm surprised you wanted to wait so long for the keepsakes. I know what these mean to you."

"I needed a few days to ensure that I could meet you without being tracked," he explained, his tone back to the near inflectionless android tone she remembered from their earliest meetings. "Hiding a conversation is easier than hiding physical objects. Plus, you have to understand bureaucracy. I've worked for the government for decades, so I understand."

She furrowed her brow in confusion. "What does the understanding of bureaucracy have to do with anything?"

"Once blindsided, a bureaucracy is like a turtle on its back. The Navy and the PDA both have to deal with numerous questions as to why this wasn't followed up before. People have come forward with old sightings." The corner of his mouth twitched into something that might generously be called a smile. "So many dangerous and impressive things happen these days, but everyone loves a good mystery, especially one that involves magic. Now that the media's all over it, everyone wants to know about the mysterious ghost ship that doesn't exist in official Naval records—one that had obviously been exposed to a hell of a lot of magic."

He raised a hand. "The less you tell me about how the media got that information so quickly, the better. It'll avoid me having to lie to anyone at the PDA, but I do find it interesting that a local reporter was able to find out about the *Constantinople* so rapidly that she already knew key details when the government was still trying to discover what the ship actually was. That's impressive journalism from a nonmagical."

Alison wiggled her eyebrows. "That's reporters for you. They're always hungry for a scoop. Besides, most men on that ship didn't even know what was going on. Abner didn't like what happened either. Burying the truth was an insult to those brave sailors. I can understand it being hidden during the war and that no one could tell the truth when magic still had to be sealed, but the gates are open now. All the dirty little secrets need to come out, so I didn't see a problem with whispering a few things to certain people."

Agent Latherby studied her appraisingly. "I won't lie, Miss Brownstone. Under normal circumstances, if I didn't have a personal investment in this matter, I might debate what you said about the need to know. I'm well-aware that makes me a hypocrite, but be that as it may, I thank you for what you've done. I would never have been able to accomplish this, even if I were to attempt it myself. You're right. The keepsakes and legacy of what they represent are important to me."

She retrieved the locket and watch from her pocket, set

them on the table, and slid them toward him. "You should be proud, Agent Latherby. You come from a legacy of service. Your great-grandfather fought to the end to protect his country and those he cared about. He didn't give up until he completed his mission."

The man picked the watch up and stared at it, a reflective look in his eyes. "I've always known he was a great man. Somehow, I knew, but now I have proof." He stood and offered her a slight nod. "I don't wish to be rude, but I think I should return to the office. Given our caution in this matter, I doubt you'll receive any pressure from the government. They'll want it to go away as soon as possible, and there's little significant reason to harass you over something that wasn't even illegal."

Alison picked her cup of tea up. "And what if they ask you?"

"Some secrets are worth keeping, even from the PDA."

Her grin was a little challenging. "Careful, Agent Latherby. You're turning into my dad."

"There are worse things in this world."

CHAPTER SEVENTEEN

Rasila settled into her chair across from Alison's desk, a knowing smile on her face. Five minutes earlier, she had called for a meeting, not bothered to assume her human disguise, and simply portaled to the front of the building and marched inside. The lack of stealth didn't bother either of them. There wasn't a Drow left who didn't understand that Rasila and Alison were close allies, and everyone on Earth knew Alison was half-Drow. Her adoption trial made sure of that.

"I apologize for the delay, Alison," the princess began with a flick of her wrist. "I needed time to confirm more information before I met with you to make plans. It was useful to know Marat was a traitor, as that does add to some of the efforts of my other spies." She frowned. "At least the surviving ones. Drae might have openly struck at you, but she's attempting to blind my network instead of attacking me directly. I don't know if that means she considers you or me the greater threat, but that doesn't matter. What we do know is she's now ready to make her move."

Alison nodded. "After what happened before, I made my mind up to see this through to the end, one way or another. Having assassins arrive to kill me when I'm in the middle of other business only makes me want to get it over with. Drae screwed up. She must have really thought that guy could succeed. I almost feel bad for her. He wasn't much of a challenge, even with the artifact. I could probably have taken him and all his friends easily even without Mason."

Rasila folded her hands in her lap. "I doubt she actually believed he could win against you. Drae is arrogant but she's not an idiot. She's certain to have thoroughly investigated your capabilities. I suspect the attack was a trap for me."

"Huh? How is an artifact-empowered assassin targeting me a trap for you?" She shook her head as if that would clarify things.

The other woman raised her hand and chanted a spell. Ghostly images of a half-dozen Drow men and women appeared behind her.

"These are all spies of mine who have died in the last week," she explained. Her jaw clenched.

She likes to act as if she's above it, but she cares about her people as much as I care about mine. That's always good to see.

The Drow princess relaxed slowly and took a deep breath. "They all died after they started looking deeper into the assassination attempt. Drae's always been a worthy foe in that sense. She might have hoped that Marat would be lucky and kill you, but I think she mostly wanted to flush my people out in a way that it would take a few deaths before I realized what was happening and countered her." She pounded her fist on the surface so hard, the entire desk rattled. "She's bested me temporarily, and the only reason I'm not filled with rage over it is because she'll die very, very soon at our hands."

"If this is you calm, I don't want to see you angry." Alison shrugged. "We could stop dancing around. I'm at the point where I'm more than happy to go to her and end this shit once and for all. She only got away with it last time because I didn't want innocent people hurt, but unless she's camped in a stadium twenty-four-seven, she's vulnerable."

Rasila smiled. "Ah, the Princess of the Shadow Forged again proves she's more Drow than human, despite her protests."

"Have you actually met any humans? Humanity isn't exactly a peaceful species."

"A good point." The princess chuckled. "But no, I don't suggest we attack Drae immediately."

"Why not?" She frowned. "It wasn't that long ago you told me we should take care of her. Why not now? She's killing your people and she tried to kill me. We're past the point of talking and hugging it out."

"Because as much as it pains me to admit it, I don't know where she is and we can't kill her unless we can locate her." Rasila waved her hand and the Drow images vanished. "All the spies I had close to her are dead, and she's not made any public appearances. Any attempts to track her magically have failed. I assume she's ensconced behind a mountain of anti-tracking spells. We can't simply gather an army and attack locations at random. I assume part of the reason she's been so focused on killing my spies despite the danger of exposing herself is that the attack on you was a prelude to her major move."

Alison sighed. "Damn it. Then what, we sit around and twiddle our thumbs? She can send an assassin every day for fun and maybe get lucky."

"In this case, yes, we do sit around." Rasila conjured another image, this time of Laena, the ex-queen. Unlike the imprisoned crone, this was the beautiful younger woman, the same one who had attempted to take Alison from her father.

She frowned. "What does she have to do with anything?"

"One piece of information that has come my way recently concerns Drae's immediate goals." The woman inclined her head toward the image. "Her plan involves freeing Laena somehow."

"Really?"

Rasila nodded. "Yes, and I'm puzzled. Everything I've heard from my spies and from Drae herself indicates that she doesn't admire Laena all that much. She paid lip service to the former queen, but I was always sure she intended to take the throne for herself."

"Laena's still strong," Alison observed. "Without the binding rituals on her, she'd easily be the single most powerful Drow and has centuries on any of us surviving princesses. Drae might simply want to serve the most powerful woman in the end. Drow strength and all that."

"It's very Drow, but it's not very Drae." Her companion's forehead creased in consternation. "Novati, yes, but Drae? She's never been overly concerned with raw power, but this knowledge still gives us a sorely needed advantage."

"How?"

"I've had to be careful with my loyal servants," Rasila explained. "I won't have such fine men and women dying for no good reason, but now that we know Drae's interested in freeing Laena, it gives us a place to watch with less risk."

She snapped her fingers. "The prison. That makes sense."

"Exactly." A vicious smile settled over the woman's face. "And this is almost too perfect. We can wait until Drae makes her move on the prison and crush her then. It won't be something she can accomplish with a small number of her forces. It'd be premature to gather an army there, let alone without knowledge of when she'll attack, but we can at least have people nearby."

The plan made sense, but something about it bothered her. It felt like they were overlooking something important.

"Won't that risk considerable collateral damage?" she asked.

Rasila shook her head. "Have you never visited the prison?"

Alison wrinkled her nose. "Why the hell would I want to do that?"

"It's in an out-of-the-way place. There are guards there, of course, but if we need to use our full strength, we won't risk innocent lives, and I guarantee you any guard at the prison is more than willing to give their lives rather than let a prisoner escape."

She considered that for a moment. "I've heard about them. They all belong to some kind of guild that swears on their honor to let no one escape."

"The Eternal Twilight." The Drow princess laughed and it sounded almost cruel. "Laena actually lavished support on them because of how effective they were at their jobs. It's a great irony that she's now their prisoner. Fortunately for her, they find torture beneath them. They believe that simply being incarcerated for centuries is painful enough and that a prisoner can reform their spirit with enough reflection in prison."

"I can't say that sounds crazy."

Rasila locked gazes with her. "We have a target and an immediate plan, but we need to discuss what happens afterward."

Alison didn't avert her eyes. "Meaning?"

"If you truly want to move the Drow forward, you should consider becoming queen."

She gave a slight nod. "I'm not saying no, but I'm not saying yes. I'm still trying to work some things out."

Her companion smiled. "Then my battle's already halfway won, but there is another thing you should consider, Princess of the Shadow Forged."

"What?"

"Your close non-Drow friends should be involved in the upcoming battles. There's no reason to leave powerful allies out of our plans."

Alison frowned. "What? You, of all people, want me to involve non-Drow in the Drow succession?"

"Yes," Rasila replied breezily. "I've thought about it because of everything that has happened. If the Drow are to move into the future, they need to become less insular. If we were the mighty, unstoppable warrior race we believe we are, a single man wouldn't have been able to humble our queen with such ease." She raised her hand and wisps of shadow formed into a rough image of James. "Being closed-off and insular has kept certain outsiders from interfering with us before, but it's now obvious that we need new blood and new perspective. Your power and success are proof of what that can bring, and it's also why Myna chose to train you."

"Okay, I understand that and I'm done not being involved, but I'm also not sure I can leave Earth entirely. I'm helping with this because I don't want Drae—let alone Laena—to be queen, but I still can't really see how that ends."

The Drow's tight smile didn't reach her eyes. It was like she knew a secret she refused to share.

"I have thoughts on that, but you're right. We need to focus on the immediate threat of Drae and Laena, and since the latter is involved, we return to the issue of your non-Drow allies. I argue that we shouldn't ignore our most powerful weapon." Her grin was chilling. "One who would never betray you."

She groaned. "You're talking about my Dad, aren't you?"

"Why not? He's a symbol of power and strength, and if there is anything the Drow respond to, it's power and strength. Ending the struggle sooner rather than later will save lives." There was a little too much glee in her eyes. "I'm not saying we have him fight all our battles. We, as Drow princesses, must show our strength and cunning to prove ourselves worthy to our people, but if Drae wants to bring Laena back, I see no reason why we shouldn't bring back the man who defeated her. It will send a message."

"I went from trying to keep out of this to getting my friends involved in a deathmatch." Alison pinched the bridge of her nose. "And now you want me to involve my friends and family in a war?"

Rasila shook her head. "Your family's already involved. Remember, this struggle flows directly from your father's actions. As for your friends, make sure you're trying to keep them away for the right reasons. If you value them as warriors, you won't dishonor them by trying to protect them." She threw a hand up to cut off the instinctive protest before it could be voiced. "It was reasonable, in previous months, to keep this a more purely Drow matter, but Drae's used so many non-Drow tools that the concept of Drow political purity is ridiculous. She's killing my people and tried to kill you. It's time to gather our allies and strike when she initiates her plan. The sooner we end this, the fewer of our people will suffer."

Her thoughts swirled in turmoil. She'd tried so hard in the past to avoid this precise scenario. It was like the harder she pulled away, the more the Drow yanked her in like some pointy-eared Mafia.

I have a duty and responsibility, exactly like Abner.

"I'll talk to my people," she replied. "I won't order them. They have to choose."

The woman nodded, the creepy grin now replaced by a look of more sober satisfaction.

Alison had other allies she could call in, including Lily and Izzie, but decided against asking them. Lily had already almost been killed by Drow machinations during their last job together. She had a separate enough existence from Alison that the Drow wouldn't target her. Izzie deserved a twenty-year vacation after what her family went through with the Seventh Order.

I have allies here at the company and among the Drow. Rasila's right. It's time to gear up and win.

CHAPTER EIGHTEEN

A rugged crag towered over Drae. Softly glowing intricate carved arcane symbols covered most of the rocks. They represented power—power and victory that would soon be hers.

My plans are coming to fruition after years of planning, ever since the fall of Laena. The others thought they were preparing but they waited, content to let the Guardians make a mockery of us all.

As she stood beneath the shadow of the mountain crag under the inky darkness of night, Drae embodied her role as Princess of the Deepest Night. The feeble light from the symbols barely illuminated the outline of her body.

Dozens of Drow in dark, hooded robes stood behind her and waited in silence for her to begin to speak. They represented the core of her supporters, the carefully selected shock troops who would begin the purification of the Drow. The others who might dare stand against her would be sacrificed to the great cause.

We have grown soft. We have grown weak. We shouldn't fear what others think. They should fear us. I will make them fear us.

She turned and her long white hair fluttered at the touch of a gust of wind.

"My loyal servants," she bellowed. "We will soon begin the plan. All is proceeding as I have foreseen. The last of the Guardians will soon be dead, and only two other princesses remain to challenge the return of the true queen."

"Forgive me, my princess," called a Drow woman. "But I heard that Marat failed."

"Yes." Drae sounded unconcerned. "He was merely a test, a gambit. I knew he would likely fail, and I believe even he knew that, but he represents what it will take to defeat the other princesses—an expenditure of blood. Effort isn't enough in war."

The woman bowed her head. "Yes, my princess."

A bear of a warrior stepped forward. "My princess, I will follow you to death, but are you sure about the plan? Must we sacrifice so many of our own people? Every Drow that dies weakens us."

A few murmurs of approval spread through the crowd. They were soon drowned out by shouts of disapproval and glares at those who dared question their princess. She silenced everyone by raising her hand.

"We are the Drow," she shouted. "We are the strong and should be the rightful rulers of Oriceran, but we have become corrupted and weak. We need to return to the old ways and achieve purity and strength. That is the only chance we have to earn the respect we deserve. Purity and strength!"

The crowd shouted their agreement in near unison, "Purity and strength!"

Drae raised her arms. Shadow wings grew from her back and purple illusionary flames erupted around her. She rose slowly into the sky. "You cannot achieve purity and strength by being merciful to those who don't wish to be strong. Do you wish to save lives or do you wish to be strong?"

"We wish to be strong, my princess!" the crowd roared.

She hovered above them, bathed in the harsh purple light of her spell. "Achieving purity and strength means casting off weakness, both magical and spiritual. We shall do that soon, and those of you who have loyally supported me will be rewarded when the new order arises. The Drow will become a power to be feared. Would you rather be loved or feared?"

"Feared!" they chanted.

The princess threw her head back and uttered a blood-curdling, primal scream. "Let all know the Drow will rise again and soon, even King Oriceran will not dare to risk our wrath. Let all who live in the light remember why they fear the darkness."

Alison smiled at the small, dark-haired baby who lay on his stomach across the room, his tiny little hands and feet pressed into the carpet. "Show me what you got, little brother. Mom claimed you could do it, but I have my doubts."

Thomas cooed and pushed himself onto his hands and knees. He crawled toward her, giggling.

Shay and James watched from the couch. The original Thomas, the family dog, lay curled in a corner asleep.

"Isn't this a little early?" she asked as her brother continued his pint-sized charge. "The crawling? He should, like, what…only be able to roll over or something."

Her mother shrugged. She tried to look nonchalant but motherly pride leaked through in a smile. "Sure, it's a little early, but it's not freakishly soon. It's not like he could sprint from the moment he was born."

Thomas reached his sister. He sat on his diapered butt, his squishy, adorable legs in front of him. "Al-Al," he cooed.

She blinked in surprise. "Is he doing what I think he is?"

Thomas giggled. "Mama. Dada. Al-Al."

Alison gasped and scooped the baby up to snuggle him. "He's talking already? You didn't tell me about this."

James grunted. "The doc says it's early but not inhumanly early. He's not strong enough to kick other babies through windows."

"I don't think that's the general standard of childhood development that most people focus on, Dad. Why didn't you tell me any of this?"

The little one yawned and rubbed his face against her shirt. His eyes drooped. "Al-Al."

"I did," Shay complained. "I told you he demonstrated faster mental and physical development." She gestured at the baby. "And that's exactly what this is."

She kissed his forehead. "Yeah, but this is a little more impressive than him being able to laugh early. If he keeps this up, he'll do parkour by the time he's two. I feel like I'll come back for Thanksgiving and he'll talk in full sentences."

"Some of this happened fairly abruptly." Her mother glanced at James. "From what he can remember, Vax kids don't necessarily grow up all that faster than humans. They live normal lives for the first few years until they are tested and bonded, so this might be a Whispy special modification. James asked him, and the sneaky little symbiont gave him some crap about basic modifications to make Thomas compatible with him."

"Big fucking deal," her dad rumbled. "Kids grow at different rates. You're both blowing this out of proportion."

Alison winced and rubbed the back of her neck. "Ah, Dad. If he's talking, maybe you should dial the cursing down. We don't need him going to preschool swearing like a...uh, Brownstone?" She shrugged.

Thomas closed his eyes and babbled something unintelligible. He stuck his thumb in his mouth.

"He's not cursing yet," James retorted. "I'll worry about it when it happens. Until then, the other kids can fuck off."

She walked over to Shay to hand the baby gently to her. "I keep going back to all this Drow sh—stuff. I know Drae needs to be eliminated, and since Laena's coming back, I definitely need to make sure she is as well. The Guardians are all but done. It's not like the Drow will turn into a democracy. I don't know if that kind of thing even makes sense for them, but if the Guardians are finished, it means the monarchy will rise again." She sat beside Shay. "This will sound arrogant, but I have the feeling if I'm not queen, things will get worse, but I'm not an idiot. There are so many nuances to Drow politics, and I'm as much a baby compared to Rasila as Thomas is to me. Even if I took over, being powerful wouldn't be enough. The whole idea is to stabilize things, not make them worse."

"Experience is overrated," James told her with a slight frown. "It's not like all these Drow actually run around and do some complicated law writing. They kick each other's ass. You already know how to do that. All this shit sounds complicated, but yeah, I get what you're saying. We tried to ignore them before and it got annoying. If you do it this time, it'll get annoying and a lot more people will die. They forced you into it."

Her mother settled Thomas into her lap and chuckled. "You're being myopic, Alison."

"How so, Mom?"

"You act like the only choices are liberal democracy or absolute monarchy." The woman stroked Thomas' hair, her affection obvious. She was a long way from the hardened killer who bragged about being willing to stab someone to death. "Even if you confine yourself to human history, there are many variations between those two poles. If you intend to be involved with them after you deal with Drae, that's what you need to think about."

Alison let her head fall on the back of the couch. "I only want to minimize the number of people who'll be hurt and make sure we're not dealing with Drow assassination attempts every few years."

"Everything you've told us about Rasila points away from anything approaching representative democracy being able to be instituted immediately," Shay mused. "The Drow simply don't want something like our government, and everything in their culture goes against it. It's not completely crazy. There is far more potential stability in a monarchy when the monarch will live for centuries. A good Drow queen means the ultimate golden age."

James grunted scornfully. "And what about when they're pieces of shit? That means they get to step on people's balls for centuries. If kings and queens were so great, nobody would have ever wanted to get rid of them."

His wife shrugged. "True, but if Alison hopes to turn the Drow government into something more like America, she'll have to think more long-term—Drow long-term. She'll have to gain political power and mold the entire society over centuries until they internalize the norms that make something like that work. Government's not magic. It's merely the set of arbitrary rules that everyone finally agrees to. When you have significant buy-in, your society can prosper. When people don't agree, civil war breaks out, and that's what we're talking about avoiding after this one is over."

Alison stared at the ceiling. Sometimes, she longed for the days of hanging out at home with James and Shay with no real responsibilities other than learning to control her power. Her summers might have been busy with training, but she never had to worry about transforming a society of people who lived for centuries.

I'm not a little girl anymore, and I'm not that helpless girl who needed James to protect her from the Harriken. I'm the Dark Princess, and it's my turn to protect people.

"All kinds of cultures have had different types of monarchs," Shay continued and her voice slipped into full professor mode. "The power of the Japanese emperor has waxed and waned over the centuries. And even in more representative governmental settings, such as a republic, different societies have come up with different rules for how to limit the power of individuals to attend to the problem your dad rather pithily stated."

She raised her head and looked at her mother. "You're saying that I can find something that pushes the Drow out of being totally reliant on the queen but still maintains stability."

Shay nodded and an eager grin appeared. "Let me give you a few books to read."

"I don't know if I'll have time to do much research, Mom."

"Fine." Her grin didn't retreat. There was nothing like sharing her passion for history with her daughter. "I'll give you a few articles. I'm not saying you should do any one thing. I merely want to give you ideas. Ultimately, this will come down to your and Rasila's decision and the support of the rest of the Drow."

James reached beneath his shirt and rubbed his thumb over his amulet. It remained separated from his skin by a metal spacer. "I want to make this shit clear. From what you've told us, if things get nasty, you might want me involved."

Alison sighed. "I don't know, Dad. I think there's some-thing to be said for using overwhelming force, but Rasilla or I have to be the one who ultimately confronts Drae. I don't know what her plan is, but it might be good to have you on standby. It's not crazy for you to deal with Laena, though. It won't introduce anything to the situation that wasn't there before."

He cracked his knuckles. "I've told you many times. If you need me to kick ass, I'll be there."

Shay frowned. "I'd help, Alison, but it's kind of hard to kill Drow and nurse at the same time." She mock-glared at her sleeping son. "Babies are a buzzkill when it comes to ass-kicking."

She laughed. "I think we've got this, Mom. I'm sure you can help during the next civil war."

CHAPTER NINETEEN

A day later, Alison walked toward the entrance to the Brownstone Building with a fresh box of bagels in her hand. She'd visited the closest local shop, but it occurred to her that as her portaling improved, the potential for special treats for the staff grew with it. It wasn't like she wanted to bring sushi from Tokyo every day, but it might be a nice treat now and then. Why bother with a taco truck when she could grab tacos from Mexico City? Even using the magic train required her to go to Starbucks and board it.

She froze outside the front door. A Drow in a long, elegant purple dress stood inside the lobby. She released a sigh of relief when the woman turned and she realized it was Rasila chatting to Ava. Some of her calm vanished, however, when she saw the serious look on the princess' face.

Clutching the bagel box a little tighter, she opened the door and stepped inside.

Ava took it from her. "Princess Rasila requests a meeting, Miss Brownstone. From what she tells me and based on our previous conversations on this matter, the meeting should also include Jerry."

She frowned. "Is Drae making her next move already?"

Rasila offered her a lazy smile. "Let's be efficient about this. Bring those you trust and we'll discuss what I know, but I wouldn't plan anything else for a while."

Ten minutes later, all the Brownstone magicals, including Sonya, sat around the conference room table, along with Ava and Jerry. Rasila stood near the front and surveyed those gathered with a mixture of amusement and condescension on her face. She'd not tried to kill anyone at the company in a long time, but that didn't mean she accepted that they were her equals. Wanting the Drow to modernize and washing away her own years of accreted old thinking were two separate things.

She might be my friend but that doesn't mean she's not a bitch.

"Despite Drae's attempts to purge my spies," Rasila began, "she hasn't succeeded in unearthing all of them. One has confirmed that some of her minions have been seen near Laena's prison, but another has also related that she is preparing a second force for some reason. They've been unable to uncover all the details, but they are sure it isn't related to freeing Laena and they assure me there will be a definitive assault on a location other than the prison."

"Damn," Alison replied. "That makes things harder but it does make sense."

"Oh? Why do you say that? I was slightly surprised to hear it myself."

"Think about it. Laena's not all that popular. I don't have to be an expert in Drow mindreading to know that. If the general Drow population loved her so much, they would have deposed the Guardians years ago. So there has to be something else Drae will do—something that will bolster Laena's popularity before she reinstalls her on the throne. We merely need to find that out."

Mason frowned. "Are you sure Laena's not popular? It could simply be that people were afraid of the Guardians. Remember the crap they pulled. Even if Drae manipulated them into it, that proves that they were more than willing to do shady stuff behind the scenes."

Rasila uttered a mocking laugh. "Afraid of the Guardians? No, that's not it. They begrudgingly respected the Guardians, but the group has never been able to generate fear. As for the idea that they manage expert schemes behind the scenes, it's laughable. They always lacked sufficient guile. It's not that they were above it morally. They were merely incompetent." She shook her head. "No, Alison is correct. Few yearn for the lost days of Laena. For all her power, she was sadistic and erratic. The Drow value guidance and strength, not mindless cruelty. She'd forgotten what it meant to be queen." She frowned. "I understand how a simple-minded woman such as Novati would support Laena, but Drae is too intelligent for that. I don't understand why she's so interested in freeing her. Why willingly give up power to a woman who has already proven too foolish to rule?"

Not too weak. Merely too stupid. She did piss my dad off. That's top of the stupidity list.

"It doesn't matter," Alison replied. "Unless it's some kind of trick?"

"I've considered that, but I don't understand her ultimate goal."

Jerry looked from one princess to the other, slight discomfort on his face. "Alison, aside from you, I don't know Drow from wombats, but this kind of reminds me of…" He grimaced. "Sorry, it kind of reminds me of a mob war."

Hana laughed and slapped her knee. "Alison's so gangster." She gasped. "That makes me what—Gangster Fox?"

Rasila gave him a lop-sided grin. "Organized crime is often similar to the Drow. Both groups value strength in their leaders but I presume, human, that you have some other point than mere comparison?"

He nodded. "Back when I was a cop, most of the times when there was an internal struggle in an organization, it wasn't a one-and-done kind of deal. Simply killing a guy isn't enough. There are always those who remain loyal to the old boss. Often, you saw a series of murders beforehand or coordinated attacks around the same time."

Alison frowned. "That makes painfully too much sense. It might explain why she's setting up a second force. She intends to move on Rasila and me directly, but she…" She looked at the other Drow princess before she returned her gaze to Jerry. "That strategy makes sense, but she'd have to neutralize both Rasila and me almost simultaneously, which means she would need three forces. We actually have control of more Drow loyal to us than she has."

"One of the groups might split later." He shrugged. "It's not like I never split my team on a job."

"There's only so much mobility, even with magic, and Drae could do considerable damage very quickly. Depending on who or what she targets, that could be a big problem. We need to know where she'll strike."

Sonya raised her hand timidly. "M-may I speak?"

Rasila sighed and rolled her eyes.

Alison frowned at the Drow. "If you have something useful, feel free to share. This is my first struggle for the throne. You probably know as much as I do about this kind of thing."

The girl swallowed and turned to Tahir. He nodded to encourage her.

"New Order Dynasty Infinite Three Kingdoms Wars IV." Her face turned scarlet and she began to inspect her fingers.

Drysi snorted. "Sometimes, I have no fucking idea what Americans are saying. I understand each of those words on their own, but they make no sense strung together."

"At least we're waging war on vowels." Hana winked.

The witch muttered something in Welsh. Alison didn't need to know the language to understand that the response was foul.

"I don't think any of us quite understand you, Sonya," she explained quietly. "Can you explain what you mean?"

"It's the latest game in a VR strategy series," she explained. "I've been playing it lately." She stared at the table for a few seconds before she forced her head up and made eye contact with her boss. "You choose a general who is fighting to unify China during the Three Kingdoms Period."

"I know a decent amount about that period. Mom was really into it. What does that have to do with the Drow?"

"Oh, sorry." The girl took a few quick breaths. "This whole situation reminds of the game—a group of honorable, strong warriors fighting for the crown, but I remember something from last week that might be helpful. Um…like, there are many different stats in the game. Several of them add or subtract from this stat Mandate of Heaven, and if you earn enough, it'll help you become emperor. But the thing about the game is that you can play in different ways. One way to do better is to get people in different places on your side by helping them—like protecting them from bandits or giving them stuff. But, there's a different way to do things. You can get the Mandate of Heaven also through simply scaring the crap out of people. There was this one time I played as Cao Cao, and I was, like, 'Woah, man, I'll raze this entire city, and the next city surrendered before my army even arrived.' They were all, like, 'Please glorious, Cao Cao, we pledge our eternal loyalty.'" She slapped a hand over her mouth and looked down.

Tahir put his fist to his face and politely coughed. "The source of the idea aside, there's some validity to what she's saying."

"Power through terror," Rasila uttered, a thoughtful look in her eyes. "That would make sense. It's also something Drae would enjoy. Maybe that's why she supports Laena. They're both needlessly sadistic."

"The attack would have to be in Drow territory," Alison

concluded. "If she attacked Earth, other Oricerans would be forced to respond or the treaties might be broken. She obviously won't attack other Oricerans. If she did, some of those troops King Oriceran has wandering around allegedly training might move in."

Rasila scoffed. "The Light Elves and the others will do everything they can to not be involved. There's too much concern about the collapse of the Great Treaty."

Jerry frowned. "She might not attack Earth, but if she destroyed the Brownstone Building, I wonder if the government would even care."

"You think they might attack here?" Alison's jaw clenched. She wanted to believe Drae wouldn't dare to do that, but she had fought another Drow princess and made public threats against Drae. She could easily see the government might use that as an excuse why they wouldn't retaliate if the attack was limited in scope. They could argue that she had brought it on herself.

Does Drae understand Earth politics well enough to pull that off?

"Maybe," she concluded. "Which means no matter what I do, I'll need to leave people here. But I can't imagine that destroying my house or building would be enough to impress all the Drow."

Ava cupped her chin, her smooth brow lined in deep thought. "Are there any settlements in Drow territory that are considered more loyal to Miss Brownstone or Princess Rasila? The rapid destruction of a loyalist settlement would set a good precedent of terror if Miss Myer's theory is correct."

Rasila shook her head. "It's not like that. Forces are

spread throughout Drow territory. I've begun the process of gathering those loyal to Alison and myself, but there is no individual place that could be destroyed that could be said to be cleanly aligned with us. Most of our warriors are gathered from various places, and the bulk of the population is simply waiting to see what happens. And even many of those are willing to fight on our behalf, but that's not the same thing as all working closely together. Some have pledged direct loyalty to Alison and some to me. Others will support us in memory of Novati and Miar. Not all who served the others have pledged to our cause, though. Many Novati supporters now serve Drae."

"Like Marat," Hana announced. "Until Alison wasted his punk ass."

Rasila smirked. "Indeed."

Alison folded her arms. If they prepared correctly, they might be able to end this civil war with a few quick, decisive battles.

"We know Laena's a big target," she suggested. "That means we should position a decent number near the prison to stop them. Rasila, if there's any way we can talk our way out of this with Drae, I'd like to hear it. No matter how quickly this goes down, people will inevitably die, and I want as few people killed as possible."

"Even if they're your enemies?" Rasila asked.

She gave a firm nod. "You were my enemy once. So were Hana and Drysi. Today's enemy can be tomorrow's friend. I won't kill people for the sake of killing."

The princess's mouth quirked into a cold smile before it settled into a flat line. "If it were so simple, Alison, this would have ended a long time ago. You've already seen what Drae is willing to do."

"I understand. I get it. Some people only understand force. It's not like I talked the Seventh Order out of being assholes, but that puts us back to our original problem. We can gather forces but we still have to deploy them. There are only so many people we can get through portals at one time." She stood and braced herself against the table with her arms. "Before we continue, I need to make something clear. The Drow who have pledged to me are one thing. This is their war, and although I would appreciate everyone's help in this, I won't order anyone from the company to participate."

Jerry shook his head. "Alison, I know I speak for almost everyone on my team when I say we'd follow you to hell if the devil spat on you and you wanted to punch him in the balls."

Mason smiled. "I'm your husband and I'm a bodyguard. I need to guard your body."

"This is like a kickass fantasy story," Hana added excitedly.

Drysi shrugged. "I have nothing to do. The vowel forces are in retreat so I might as well hunt Drow in the meanwhile."

"I want to help," Sonya murmured.

Tahir scoffed. "I'm disappointed I couldn't be more helpful during the most recent job. I think I need to remind the world of who I am."

Rasila looked from person to person. "You have loyal subordinates, Alison."

"No, Rasila." She sat once more. "I have good friends." She nodded to her assistant.

"Miss Brownstone anticipated that many of you would like to be involved. There are legal complexities involved with moving between Earth and Oriceran without formal paperwork. I've made arrangements for the core magical team." Ava adjusted her glasses and turned to Jerry. "I don't have everything finished for everyone on your team. There's also the concern that if we bring the entire Brownstone Security team, we will accrue additional undue government attention that might be difficult to escape."

His nostrils flared. "Level with me. Do you think there's a good chance this Drow bitch will attack Brownstone Security?"

"I think it's a strong possibility," Rasila replied. "She's ruthless. I'd err on the side of caution. It's better to leave some men behind than let your other people be slaughtered."

"This is only one building," he commented. "It's easy to defend one location if you know the enemy is coming. If I have my teams armed and ready to go and we have infomancer support, we can hold this building, Alison. The government might try to blame you later, but if a big Drow force arrives, I doubt AET and the PDA would let them do whatever the hell they want."

"I can stay behind," Tahir suggested.

Sonya gave a firm nod, determination etched into her face. "Me too. I'll bust them like I'm Liu Bei and this is the Battle of Red Cliffs."

Warmth spread through Alison. After leaving the School of Necessary Magic and with Izzie on the run, she wasn't sure she would ever find a group of people she could trust so completely. Now, everyone was willing to go to war for her. She wouldn't let them down.

"I think it's time to gather our Drow forces, Rasila," she suggested.

The other princess lowered her head. "Indeed it is, Princess of the Shadow Forged."

She grinned. "And I think I have an idea of how to keep Laena in check without having to divide most of our forces. A little insurance policy."

Your move, Drae.

CHAPTER TWENTY

Sweet strawberry flavor coated Alison's tongue. She shuddered in pleasure and held her cup of frozen yogurt up.

"You have to try some of this," she declared. "I think it's some of the best frozen yogurt I've ever had."

Sienna eyed it with suspicion from behind the front desk at Brownstone Security. "I don't know, Alison. I don't think I'm ready for a relationship with yogurt. My boyfriend might object."

She laughed. "Okay. So I'm exaggerating a lit—" She summoned a shadow blade as a familiar sensation filled the area. "Put everyone on alert, Sienna, and get out of here."

The girl tapped a command into the keyboard, stood, and ran into the hallway.

A portal formed a few yards away. Alison shoved magic into shield spells and marched toward it.

A shrill alarm activated. Shouts and heavy footfalls filled the building. Hana sprinted down the hallway, already foxed out, and her nine tails of light fluttered behind her. The *tachi* was in her hand. Mason and Drysi were there moments later with their wands, along with several of Jerry's team and security guards, their rifles at the ready.

No one will destroy this building.

A female Drow warrior emerged, clad in tight black armor. Bloodstains, deep cuts, and burns covered the armor. Alison recognized her as a Miar loyalist who had pledged to support her after the other princess's death.

The woman dropped to one knee. "Princess Rasila requests your aid, Princess Alison. Everything happened too quickly. Princess Drae's forces have launched their attack. Somehow, they've disrupted portals, scrying, and communication throughout the city. She's rallied most of our forces and they're attempting to defend the city."

"City?" Alison lowered her shadow blade. "You mean they didn't attack the prison?"

The Drow nodded. "Yes, they did, but they're also assaulting the capital." The woman's jaw clenched. "They've already slaughtered the remaining Guardians. It appears they aren't only attacking anyone known to be pledged to you and Princess Rasila. They're laying waste to the capital, and not only Drow forces. Zain are aiding them."

Son of a bitch.

"What's a Zain?" Hana asked.

"Nasty bastards," she explained. "Magical mercenaries. My dad's fought them before. They enjoy killing people and they're good at it." She shook her head. "So much for Drow purity. My team will come and reinforce the capital. We'll go directly to the edge of the city and we'll send a message to the prison forces to have them reinforce the city. Whatever Drae's done can't extend everywhere."

The woman looked confused. "But what about the prison? You intend to let them free Laena?"

"Nope. I have a better idea, and Princess Rasila already knows about it. We don't need an army there with my idea, and if she's simply murdering people in the streets to establish her terror credentials, we'll need all the help we can get. That means we need to throw everything we have to reinforce Rasila." She yanked her phone out and dialed.

"Yeah?" James answered. "What's up?"

"Dad, I need your help. I need you to kick Laena's ass."

"It's about fucking time."

CHAPTER TWENTY-ONE

A lison and her team emerged from her second portal near the edge of the city and beside the Drow road made of a shiny substance reminiscent of obsidian. She'd sent her father to the prison, confident that he'd be more than able to handle whatever Drae might throw at him. She'd confirmed the messenger's report by attempting to portal closer to Rasila's last known location, but magical interference stopped her.

How the hell did Drae block portaling and communications over most of the city? I know this place isn't exactly LA, but come on!

Glowing towers of dark crystal glass stood above smaller, wider wooden buildings. Several towers lay toppled and cracked and huge holes marred others. Thick smoke poured into the sky. Bright fires danced all around the city, but most of the damage seemed to be concentrated on the opposite side of the city from the palace.

So you don't want to damage your new house, Drae?

Loud booms and explosions sounded from all around.

Several Drow lay nearby, their bodies burned almost beyond recognition. Other nearby corpses had been ripped to pieces. While all Drow were powerful magically and strong compared to a typical human, that didn't mean all spent as much time practicing battle magic as the dedicated warriors did. A Drow craftsman wouldn't last a minute against a trained fighter.

A mob of four-armed monsters, each large enough to tower over her father, marched from between two smoldering buildings. Blood dripped from the razor-sharp claws of several of them.

So, it wasn't Drow who killed the people in this part of the city.

"Zain." Alison hissed a warning. "We were supposed to come out near Rasila's force, even accounting for targeting the edge of the city. Shit. I keep forgetting I've not mastered the damned spell yet."

Hana drew her sword. "This is easy, right? Kill the monsters and head to Rasila."

Drysi yanked out two red glowing daggers with a huge grin. "Finally, no stupid narrow boat halls I have to worry about and ruthless killers who have it coming."

"Don't try to go close with these guys if possible," her boss advised. "Their claws are inherently anti-magic. They can shred shields like cardboard but they don't regenerate much. They stay down."

The fox shrugged. "I'll pick off whoever gets close. I assume they die if you chop their head off?"

"Yeah."

"Easy-peasy." The woman gave a thumbs-up.

"My first civil war. I feel like there should be maudlin

fiddle music playing in the background." Mason drew his gun. They'd all loaded anti-magic rounds before leaving Earth. While it would be an expensive battle, it would help to keep her people alive.

The Zain mob released piercing, inhuman screams and attacked the team, raising their four arms in preparation to savage their opponents.

"Bring it, you bastards!" Drysi cackled and quick-tossed two daggers. They exploded in the Zain front line, charred several of the monsters, and hurled others to the ground. Mason opened fire. It took a couple of good headshots to fell his first target. Alison shoved her palms forward and her explosive light orbs streaked into the advancing Zain.

One attacker emerged from the smoke of the blasts and shrieked as it barreled toward the Brownstone team, even more frantic than before. Hana sprinted forward and sliced its head off without even slowing. She circled toward her team as they continued to unleash doom into the magical mercenaries.

These were the kind of things the Council used, Alison remembered. *And anything they used is worth killing.*

More Zain screams answered the cries of the dying creatures in front of them. The monsters spilled out in greater numbers from alleys and streets. Several emerged from a nearby tower, coated in blood. Alison switched from orbs to launching shadow crescents. The magic carved through the targets with enormous effect. Drysi threw a dagger to her side with an almost lazy motion, but the eruption decimated three mercenaries.

Hana rushed a small squad of the enemy that approached from the side. She ducked the claws of the first monster and stabbed into his side as she raced past. A sweep of her blade decapitated another. The survivors converged on her, but she danced out of the reach of their claws and grinned as she hacked and carved through them.

"You're too slow," she taunted.

Alison conjured wings and took to the skies, flying low over the Zain to draw their attention. They leapt up, tried to claw her, and only missed by inches. She didn't retaliate immediately and instead, took a few seconds between passes to fuel a large crackling white ball of magical energy. With the spell charged, she spun and launched it into the middle of their formation. The massive blue-white explosion consumed several of the enemy.

Mason holstered his gun and pulled his wand out. His follow-up attack of ice lances formed almost instantly and ripped into his targets. They toppled and fell as obstacles for the others. She rarely saw him cast so quickly and with so little effort.

I keep forgetting what it's like to be on Oriceran. This isn't a trickle of magic from barely open gates or even the stored magic of a kemana but a planet bathed in it. I feel like I could do this all day.

She divebombed the enemy. The constant attacks from the team had reduced the deadly mob to a few stragglers, but that didn't make them any less dangerous. One leapt to the side and survived one of Drysi's explosions, then barreled toward her with a fearsome screech, intent on revenge. The fox and her tails passed in front of the witch as a blur of light and a second later, the Zain fell in two halves, his legs separated from his body.

"Thanks, Hana," the witch called.

She saluted. "This doesn't mean I support your vowel war."

Drysi grinned. She'd used about half her daggers and now retrieved her wand. A quick incantation conjured a large fireball that charred the front of a brave Zain. The burned body tumbled to join the pile of others.

A group of twenty Drow, all clad in dark armor, sprinted down the street from behind the mercenaries.

Shit. Drae reinforcements? These guys won't be so easily defeated.

A wave of dark orbs and shadow crescents ripped from the Drow force into the rear of the Zain. Now pinned on both sides, the monsters had no chance as the Brownstone team and the new arrivals finished their brutal pincer attack.

Alison landed quickly and waited for the warriors to approach.

A woman stepped forward and bowed her head. Blood coated most of her armor, and she was missing a large chunk of the protection near her abdomen. Deep claw marks ran down the breastplate and her greaves. "I am Zana, Princess Alison. I served Princess Miar, and I have pledged to follow you since her death."

"Where's Rasila?" she asked.

"The princess is leading the bulk of our forces against an army of Drae's warriors. The Zain appeared and the city guard went to engage them, but then Drae's army arrived." Zana pointed to a bright flash in the distance. "With her people using countermagic to disrupt portals and messages, it's been difficult."

"Yeah." She hissed in frustration. "Damn it. We saw it

coming and they still caught us with our pants down. I need to reinforce Rasila, but I understand that you are dealing with these four-armed freaks. Can one of you lead me to her?"

Zana bowed. "I will, my princess." She motioned for her squad to move. "Continue your patrols. Death to the Zain and death to traitors who serve the murderous Drae."

The whole situation was absurd. While the Drow, like most Oriceran races, lacked the population of humanity, there was something bizarre about the tiny armies of competing princess loyalists, a few thousand Drow at most, determining the future of an entire people.

No. It was even worse than that. It might come to a handful of people.

CHAPTER TWENTY-TWO

S ometimes a man, even when retired, needed to revisit his past. James had always known the Drow situation would raise its head again. He hadn't known when it might happen, but he knew it would have to end with him reminding the Drow that there was a reason they should have never screwed with a Brownstone.

Yeah, it's time to settle this shit, he thought. He strode forward in his silver and green biometallic armor, his body and head completely covered. His symbiont was already bonded, and a blade extended from both clawed arms. He hadn't even had to sacrifice an artifact or get angry for the transformation into extended advanced mode. Whispy wasn't a magical creature but had adapted to feed on magic. The energy infused even the air of Oriceran.

Kill the enemy, he sent and glee colored his thoughts. *Maximum adaptation likely already achieved against probable attack types. Maximize efficiency for tactical practice. High levels of external energy available.*

Yeah. I could probably go full Forerunner here, but this shit's already gonna cause enough of an interplanetary incident. I'd better keep it dialed down. That'll make it easier to tell the government to fuck off if they complain later.

They'd already contacted Senator Johnstone to give him a head's up. He'd promised to keep the American government off their backs, providing they kept the disruption in Drow territory. That was fine by him. He didn't have to worry about the rest of the idiots. He only cared about whoever might arrive at the prison.

Secondary concerns irrelevant, Whispy responded. *Demonstrate superiority of adaptation and destroy all enemies with maximum efficiency.*

A red metal tower spiraled into the sky. It stood in the center of a crater-filled mess of dark, jagged rocks and toxic vapor. Gases rose from pools of thick yellow liquid all around the tower. The light of the day didn't fall directly on the structure. From a distance, the entire building looked bent as if he looked at it through water.

It must be some magic shit. Whatever. I don't care.

An explosion blew a wall out a quarter of the way up. Two bodies pitched out and plummeted to the ground.

Fuck. Everyone's in such a damned hurry. I just got here.

James crouched and vaulted upward, and his armored legs launched him at tremendous speed. He couldn't fly like his daughter, but his massive leap ended up functionally the same over short distances. He hurtled toward the new hole and didn't bother to charge a cannon blast. Creating trouble for Alison by killing the wrong people would make holidays awkward. It was advisable that he should see someone before he tried to kill them.

He landed inside the cavity with a resounding thud

against the hard rock that formed the floor of the tower. Several Drow lay on the ground with holes through their hearts or missing their heads. Whenever he'd fought a Drow before, they'd been a bitch to kill, but from what Alison had told him, that was because he'd only dealt with elites. If every member of the entire race was as tough as her or Laena, they would have conquered Oriceran millennia before.

Six others stood with shadow blades, spread out in the circular floor to surround two bleeding Drow. The two men guarded a narrow spiraling staircase that extended through the center of the chamber. Each step was a brilliant glowing amber.

Everyone looked at James and their eyes widened.

"The Queenslayer!" one of the men guarding the staircase shouted.

"I'll make this shit real easy," James rumbled, his voice transmitted automatically through his helmet. "I'm here to stop some fucks from bringing Laena back. Who supports Drae?"

The six Drow surrounding the other man glared at James.

"This isn't your affair, Queenslayer," one of them snarled. "This is a Drow matter. Leave now."

"Why? Because you told me to? Fuck that." He grunted derisively. "This shit doesn't work like that. My daughter is a Drow princess, and that bitch Laena targeted her and me before. Now, this Drae is trying to help Laena and she tried to kill my daughter a couple of times. The only reason I didn't come before and cut all you motherfuckers down is because Alison asked me not to, not because I give two shits about pissing off Drow, King Oriceran or anyone. I only give a shit about protecting my family and friends, and anyone who works for Drae isn't either of those." He sliced through the air with one of his blades. "This is your last chance, assholes. Run or die."

The six attacked with a bellowed challenge. He made no effort to dodge. They hacked at his armor with their shadow blades but the magically coalesced shadows barely nicked his protection, let alone hurt him. The few minor cuts in the armor filled before the warriors could swing again.

Maximum adaptation achieved against existing attack type, Whispy announced. *Regeneration in progress. Engage and terminate enemies. Low probability of additional adaptation.*

James sliced one apart with his first blade before he gutted another with his second. He carved the man in half to make sure he couldn't heal before he spun to kick a third. The powerful blow launched the man out of the hole and he plummeted toward certain death.

The surviving Drow leapt back and released their shadow blades. One swung his arm to launch a thick shadow crescent. The spell struck his arm and barely registered in his mind. Another chanted a spell and purple liquid splashed against his armor and sizzled.

"That's some weak-ass shit." He chuckled. "I hope you guys aren't supposed to be special forces."

Maximum adaptation achieved against existing attack types, Whispy reported. *Recommend efficient removal of enemies.*

Yeah, good advice. These guys are a waste of time.

A few more blade swings left a pile of body parts in the bloodied chamber.

James turned his head toward the two Drow who guarded the stairs. "What the fuck is your deal?"

The men bowed their heads.

"We serve the Eternal Twilight," one of the men announced.

He grunted in recognition. "Alison told me about you guys. You're like permanent prison guards."

"Yes, Queenslayer."

"You got a problem with the fact I beat Laena?" he challenged. He didn't know enough about Drow politics to even attempt to read between the lines.

"No." The man gestured to one of the bodies. "Drae's warriors have raided this prison to free the former queen. We of the Twilight are honor-bound to stop any who would free our prisoners. The warriors of Princess Rasila and Alison were aiding us, but they left."

"Yeah, because Alison sent me." He grinned. "Where the fuck is Laena?"

"Below." They pointed to the stairs. "The queen is deep in the bowels of this prison. There are ancient ruins where she is kept."

James strode over to the stairs and growled in annoyance. He'd hoped to jump to the bottom but there was no actual shaft so he would have to follow them all the way down.

"Queenslayer," shouted one of the men. "You can't simply go down. You don't have the warding stones on you. If you proceed without them, the defensive magic will attack you on different levels. You'll never survive the descent."

"Can't you give them to me?" he asked.

"We personally don't have any. The only other way is spells. They take time to cast."

"I don't have time to wait around."

Recommend purposeful triggering of security measures, Whispy sent. *Moderate adaptation potential.*

James ignored his symbiont. "If Drae's assholes already went through, I won't even have to worry about it."

"No. It's not like that. The spells can't be disabled so easily. Drae's people had warding stones." The Drow clenched his hand into a fist, his expression grim. "We don't know how they got them. We've fought them but we lack numbers, and without the defensive magic, we can't slow them."

"So, let me get this straight. I have to run through your death gauntlet and at the bottom, there are some ruins and shit, and Laena should be there?"

The Drow nodded. "Yes, but you'll never sur—"

He raced down the stairs and his heavy armored footsteps echoed through the stairwell. As soon as his head cleared the ceiling for the new level, red beams streaked from all sides and struck his armor. The attack stung and pitted the protection. Silver-green strands stretched into the pits to fill the holes.

Adaptation and regeneration in progress, Whispy reported. *Maximum adaptation now achieved against attack type.*

Four stone cubes of different colors stood against each wall of the tower. Given the size, he suspected they were cells.

Other prisoners aren't my problem, though.

Entirely focused, he continued down the stairs and

took them two or three at a time. More Drow carnage lay scattered around the new level, along with more cells.

What the fuck? he thought. *This is like fifty levels of stairs. Huh. I shouldn't be too surprised. Prisons are supposed to be annoying.*

James didn't encounter any additional living Drow as he passed through one death trap after another. Other than some crushing walls he needed to blast through, the traps did nothing but bounce off him or cause him only minor damage. It had taken him decades to gain basic proficiency with the symbiont, but once he understood how it worked, he'd spent considerable time deliberately exposing the adaptive armor to different types of attacks. Alison and Shay had helped. At this point, he wasn't sure if there were many things left on Oriceran or Earth that could threaten him. The Nine Systems Alliance probably had a few toys, but they stayed out of his way and he did his best to not attract their attention. He wasn't afraid of them, but he was worried about how willing they might be to harm innocent people to get at him.

The long trip ended when the stairwell descended into a sprawling cavern. The walls and roof of the space glowed a dull red, and he wondered if he was in something like a kemana. The Oricerans wouldn't theoretically need something like that, but there was much about the magical world he didn't understand. Unlike Alison and Shay, he didn't care about knowing its secrets. All he needed to know was whether he could survive a particular attack.

Low chanting sounded in the distance and he looked in that direction. A narrow passage led to a corridor. Several Drow bodies lay strewn about the entrance to the passage.

He marched in that direction, stopped when someone groaned, and looked down.

One of the men's eyes fluttered open, an impressive feat given that there were several baseball-sized holes completely through his chest.

"Queenslayer," he gurgled. "You must hurry. Magic... pulsing..." He coughed up blood. "They're doing some kind of ritual. Laena is...close." His head fell to the side and he took his last breath.

James jogged into the corner and bounced off an invisible wall. He growled in annoyance.

Recommend efficient destruction of barrier, Whispy sent.

"Yeah. I don't have time for this shit." He backed away and raised both arms. Green sparks lit the blades and danced and coalesced together in bright green light. Twin rays erupted forward from the blade. They struck the unseen barrier and created a vivid flash. His attack continued and pounded into the wall behind to vaporize the rock and dirt. A dark cloud billowed outward and obscured the area.

He surged into the dust cloud and turned the corner. The long, narrow path widened into another huge cavern. Dozens of Drow filled the chamber. Thirteen of them stood in the center and chanted. They surrounded another cube approximately seven feet by seven feet by seven feet and composed of solid black rock. Arcane symbols in bright white light floated above the magical cell and circled it. Other magical symbols and wards filled the sides and top of the cube.

The non-chanting Drow all walked toward him and disdain dripped from their expressions.

"Don't interfere, James Brownstone," a woman called. "Your daughter had her chance to bend her knee. She chose her course. If she begs for forgiveness, she might be spared."

Low probability of adaptation, Whispy reported, slight irritation underlying his thoughts. *Recommend rapid termination of all enemies except those surrounding cubic structure. Do not engage targets.*

Huh? Why's that?

Unknown activity in progress. Unable to evaluate new adaptation probability.

He chuckled. *You want me to let them do whatever they're doing so you can maybe learn something new?*

Achieve maximum adaptation for maximum combat efficiency, Whispy countered. *Such achievement will increase the probability of destruction of other symbiont-bound units, leading to better achievement of primary directive.*

That was Whispy Doom, always looking forward to the next fight, but he did have a point.

James didn't bother to give a speech or offer the Drow a chance to surrender. He already knew the kind of men and women they were. He raised his arms and charged his cannons. The Drow bathed him in a death wave of fireballs, acid, poison clouds, and slicing shadow crescents. They did more damage to the floor than to his armor.

He released his own death rays as he swept his arms in opposite directions. The attack cut through the Drow warriors with ease, obliterated their upper bodies, and left charred remains. Despite Whispy's advice, he didn't stop and cut through the chanting men and women, but when the rays struck the cube, they turned at a sharp angle and carved into the room above. He ceased fire when rock and dirt rained from the damaged area.

"Huh," he marveled. "It's not every day I find something that can take a direct hit from me."

It didn't matter. There wasn't a single Drow left intact, let alone alive in the entire chamber.

"That's that. Fucking Drow. Why did you have to piss Alison off?"

The magical symbols all hummed loudly. They shifted color to a deep purple and then black. The remains of the bodies caught fire. Streams of dark-blue flame streaked from the bodies and flowed toward the cube. Other fire streamed from the passage and several trails of flame burst through the roof toward the cube.

"What the fuck now?"

High level of potential adaptation, Whispy sent. *Prepare to engage and terminate enemy.*

The flows continued for about thirty seconds before they faded. A large crack slivered through the side of the cube followed quickly by another, then another.

James raised a blade. "Am I supposed to be scared of that weak-ass shit?"

The cell exploded and flung fragments in a wide radius. A few struck him and bounced harmlessly aside. A thick cloud of dust obscured his vision and he waited for it to settle. A slender female form floated where the cube had stood, naked except for the purple glow that cloaked her body.

He recognized the beautiful Drow woman with the long white hair, but the last time he had seen her, she had been a shriveled crone. Now, she looked younger than Alison.

"Laena," he said acidly. "I should have killed you when I had the chance."

The Drow queen threw her head back and laughed. "Fate smiles upon me. The creature who facilitated my imprisonment has come to be destroyed. This is too perfect."

"I remember similar ranting before." He chuckled. "How did that go for you last time?"

Eight shadow wings erupted from her back, and she ascended quickly. "I'm not what I was before. Drae took measures and arranged for me to absorb soul and life in a way I never could before. I'm more powerful than I ever was. All Drow in this tower, living or dead, have become a part of me."

"You killed everyone?" He looked at her with disgust.

"I gave them purpose."

"You fucking ate your own people's souls? You're a twisted bitch."

"Traitors!" she thundered. Her eyes turned solid black, ringed by a dark-purple glow. "My people turned their backs on me and imprisoned me. They let that half-breed traitor come and train with them. I am the Drow. It doesn't matter if every last one of them dies as long as I survive."

High probability of adaptation, Whispy sent. *Engage and kill enemy and achieve additional adaptation. Increase secondary social reputation to minimize unnecessary inefficient conflicts.*

You want me to kick her ass so I can scare away losers who won't improve you? Don't worry. I have my own reasons to want to do this, and if everyone else is dead, I don't have to hold back.

James rubbed his blades against one another. "Here's the thing, Your Royal Bitchiness. You might be tougher than the last time we fought, but guess what? So am I."

CHAPTER TWENTY-THREE

Alison and her team followed Zana through the broken streets and destroyed buildings of the city. The evidence of carnage increased in the form of bodies as they approached the main battle site. What were once distant dots became hundreds of Drow who flung spells or stabbed at each other. Rasila soared over the battle and fired a variety of magic, cutting shadow crescents, explosive orbs, and burning beams. Adversary after adversary fell, but some stood again and grimaced while shadows oozed into their wounds. The elites might be the most difficult to defeat, but every Drow warrior could heal themselves. Each fighter in the larger of the two armies wore armor with a dark purple fringe, something Alison had seen before with some of Drae's followers. That was convenient because it made them easily identifiable.

At least Drae's stylish. Our people don't even match.

The Brownstone team stood about fifty yards behind the enemy line on a wide road leading to a massive square.

The remains of a crumbled stone fountain lay scattered across the square, the obvious victim of multiple explosions. Magic could restore much, but even spells had their limits.

A rainbow riot of magic erupted in the sky around Rasila and she dropped behind the allied rear lines. A roaring cheer rose from Drae's army.

Alison's breath caught, and her gaze darted around to assess the scene. The attack wasn't enough to stop Rasila, but her forces were surrounded and penned in against a massive collapsed tower. She hissed with anger when she recognized the half-collapsed building. She should have realized what it was the minute she saw the fountain square. It was the Library of Middle Winter, one of the more important libraries in the city.

Drae intends to save the Drow by killing everyone and destroying their heritage?

"Something's wrong," she muttered. "And not only Rasila getting hurt."

"Many things are wrong, A," Mason commented. "This is a civil war."

"Princess Alison," Zana pleaded. "We must reinforce our allies. They're being overrun."

Hana drew her sword. "These Drow don't have anti-magic claws. This will be fun and easy."

Drysi twirled an explosive dagger in her fingers. "The queen is dead. Long live the queen."

Alison extended a shadow blade. "You don't understand. Where the hell is Drae? I don't see her anywhere. If she's not here, there's a reason for that and I doubt it's any good."

We knew she would try something but never imagined she would be crazy enough to indiscriminately attack the capital. We can't let her trick us again.

"What's the play?" Mason asked.

"Screw it." She snarled with real anger. "We don't have time to worry about her. We need to save Rasila and the other Drow." She summoned shadow wings and launched into flight. She didn't attack immediately and instead, took the time to swirl light and shadow magic together into a crackling white sphere of death.

Her friends and Zana attacked. No one screamed or called out in challenge. The enemy Drow were too focused on firing spells at the allied army. The Brownstone team had fought together in countless battles. While they might officially be security contractors, they had more battle experience than a good number of those in the enemy army who only had the chance to train and spar. Actual war was foreign to many of the so-called warriors.

Alison released her spell and the orb soared toward the ground. Drae's army finally realized that another princess had joined the battle, but it was too late. The explosion rippled through their lines and catapulted Drow into one another. Drysi, Mason, Zana, and Hana completed their charge and assaulted the back line.

The *tachi's* blade glinted in the sun as the fox swung and sliced. She bounded over falling bodies to carve into others. A few Drow managed a strike here and there and the red glow of her defensive artifact dimmed but didn't fail. Any chance of rallying against her vanished when Drysi blasted the army with the last few of her explosive daggers.

Zana held her hand up and her shadow blade extended into a spear. She impaled an enemy that staggered toward her and shouted in triumph. Mason chose practicality. He took careful shots with his anti-magic-loaded pistol. The bullets drilled through the enemy shields. His first victim's eyes widened in surprise as the shot ripped through him. No one, even a magical, should ever underestimate a gun.

Alison circled the enemies at high speed and winced from the counterattack, which included a pale-blue ray that burned a hole in her shoulder. She grimaced with pain, moved higher, and gave herself a moment to funnel magic to deepen the shadow in her shoulder and heal the wound.

This isn't merely a group of thugs. This is a trained Drow army.

The allied forces took advantage of the chaos in the enemy lines to surge forward and blast, hack, and cut. One enterprising Drow leapt back and shouted a loud incantation that could almost be heard over the din of battle. He slapped his hands on the tower. Several large chunks ripped from the rubble and exploded over groups of Drae's warriors to shower them with red-hot fragments.

When Alison's pain ebbed, she flipped and conjured small spheres of light that began to orbit her. The spell wasn't something she'd used much, but Mason had a few times, and she'd liked the idea and developed a variant during recent training. She continued to dart and zig-zag across the sky while she added new spheres to the orbit. Her greater raw magical ability let her stack even more for maximum burst capability.

Rasila launched upward and drew some of the fire away from her. The other princess didn't immediately attack. Instead, she focused on erratic maneuvers and defensive spells, which included launching several small dark clouds that erupted into dark confetti that absorbed blows like magical chaff.

Damn. I'm way more relieved than I thought I'd be that she's okay. Now, the momentum's on our side, but Drae had to know we'd come to help Rasila. There must be some other card she'll play.

Alison took her opportunity and dove toward the enemy forces. One of her spheres launched into the crowd and exploded into smaller ones like a magical shotgun. The spell shredded her opponent's shields with ease and blew dozens of holes in the unfortunate warriors. She released the remainder of her spells and perforated several more.

Hana and Zana stood back to back and thrust and sliced their way through their confused adversaries. Drysi had run out of explosive daggers and chose Mason's practical anti-magic bullet approach but even Alison's largesse had limits. He had long since run out of the bullets and now kept his distance while his wand pelted quick-chant fireballs at the enemy.

After a quick glance to satisfy herself that her team was fine, she flew toward Rasila.

"Welcome, Princess of the Shadow Forged," the princess shouted. "I would have preferred better timing, but I won't lie and claim I was untroubled by the battle."

Alison surveyed the battlefield. Before, Drae's force had all but enveloped the allied forces but now, they were encircled by Alison's team on one side and the Drow army on the other. It was obvious that a member of the Brownstone team was worth a good ten of the Drow warriors. Not only that, but the vicious aerial assaults had disrupted their lines.

The losses among the enemy army were staggering and the allied forces now outnumbered them.

"Where the hell is Drae?" she yelled.

The other princess laughed, the merry sound strange given the death below them. "A coward to the end, but I'd assume with her other army."

"Other army?" She groaned. "There's another army?"

"Yes. Shortly before this battle began, a messenger informed me that her forces had another, smaller army in a different part of the city, but I couldn't risk dividing my forces and this one was killing other Drow." Rasila wrinkled her nose in disgust. "Only a coward cuts down non-warriors to prove their strength. I'll enjoy killing Drae."

"It's a good thing I called most of our forces from the prison. I don't know how long it'll take with the limited number of portal-capable Drow in the group, though. Also, we have no idea how close they can come with Drae blocking portaling throughout the city."

"You recalled the prison forces?" Rasila threw her head back and howled in delight. "I see. You sent the Queenslayer into battle."

"Don't call him that. He's my dad." Alison dodged a flaming arrow and replied with a few shadow crescents.

"We have the upper hand," her fellow princess declared. "Let's crush the rest of this army and we can connect with our reinforcements and drive Drae from her hiding place. Then, we can taunt her. Whatever scheme she had concocted to reinstall Laena is doomed. I'm sure the Queenslayer has killed all Drae's men already, and Laena will continue to rot in her prison."

CHAPTER TWENTY-FOUR

James gestured for Laena to attack. He had to ignore the constant chatter in his head from Whispy, demanding that he initiate the battle. "Come on. Turn into your killer jellyfish or whatever that shit was you did last time. I don't want this to drag on." He wanted Laena to understand exactly how outclassed she was.

The queen offered him a vicious smile. "I'll give you one chance, James Brownstone. Come to me. Kiss my feet and ask my forgiveness. I could use a man of your power. If you pledge to be my warrior, I won't destroy you and I'll give your daughter a place at my side. After all the time she spent rejecting us, she's here fighting now. She should have simply come to us before."

"You wanted to take her from me, don't you remember?"

"The situation has changed and the Drow always respect power."

He scoffed. "You sure know a lot for someone who was locked up all these years."

"The truly loyal never forgot their queen," Laena replied. She raised her hand. Purple lighting blasted from her and struck him squarely and fiery pain erupted in his chest.

He staggered back with a grunt and a charred hole in his armor.

Yesss, Whispy cheered. *New adaptation in progress. Regeneration in progress.*

"Interesting." She raised a slender eyebrow. "You have improved. I'm sure that attack would have killed the old you. Now I want you more than ever. My loyal dog. My James Brownstone."

"My turn." He ignored the agony that suffused his chest, but the pain had already begun to fade as the wound mended and the gap in the armor sealed itself. He pointed his arm and collected energy before he fired an energy ray. The green beam streaked into Laena and burned through her chest.

She looked at the hole where her lungs and heart used to be and then at him. Deep shadows tinged with purple filled the holes before they faded to reveal fresh skin. She uttered a thunderous, mocking laugh.

"Did you really think such a feeble attack would defeat me? I must admit to a mild curiosity as to whether or not you had grown, but now I see it is nothing but boasting."

"It's not a boast if you can back it up." He leapt toward her. Shadows swallowed her arms and they became undulating tenebrous whips. One cracked against his blade.

Sampling in progress, Whispy reported.

The other lashed into him and careened him back. He

impacted with a cavern wall, unhurt, and dropped onto his feet.

Maximum adaptation already achieved against attack type, Whispy assured him, a cheerful undercurrent to the thought.

James growled in irritation. "Now you're pissing me off. I could be at home playing with my son and eating barbecue, but I'm over here on this twisted-ass planet dealing with someone I already beat down. You won't go to prison this time, Laena. You're dead."

"I will destroy you, James Brownstone," she shouted, her voice guttural and distorted. "You are nothing before me now." The purple-tinged shadows spread from her arms to the rest of her body. Her form contorted and grew. Her legs split in two, and her arm divided into eight massive whip-like tentacles. Any hint of her face or female form had vanished. Irregular blotches of dark purple covered the blackened shadowy form. The massive body would have dwarfed his F-350.

"What the fuck are you doing now?" he called. "Is this your idea of coming on to me?"

"Power is everything, James Brownstone. You, of all people, should understand that." When Laena spoke, several different overlapping voices emerged, different tones and pitches like a dissonant, twisted choir. "You proved that before when you defeated me. I looked weak and my people betrayed me but now, their sacrifices have made me strong. I will destroy all who oppose me until no one is left but those who serve their queen."

"Even if you could win against me, I'm fairly sure the

Great Treaty says something about gobbling people's souls like they were pulled pork."

Her entire form shook and the tentacles swayed as she laughed, the sound harsh and alien. "The Great Treaty is nothing. Once I defeat you, I can continue to feast. I will rule Oriceran. The king will pledge to serve me or I will destroy him as well."

"You know what your problem is?" James challenged.

"Your arrogance and interference?"

"No. You should have been satisfied with what you had. It's why I only have the one restaurant. Me, I get it. I need one restaurant. If I wanted more, I'd start doing stupid shit like cutting corners. The meat would suffer."

"How could I have been defeated by such a pathetic creature?" Laena screeched. "That's what you've become? An innkeeper."

"No. I'm a pitmaster."

The entire cavern shook. A swirling purple cloud of particles surrounded one of the tentacles. It spread to the other eight and exploded as a writhing mass toward him. The force of the wave blasted dirt and rock into a dense cloud. The purple-hued mass hurled into him a nearby wall. He snarled in response to the attack and shook his head. Eight bolts of black lightning fired from Laena's tentacles and converged on him. The debris from the explosion blinded him.

New adaptation achieved, Whispy declared. *Adaptation and regeneration in progress. Prioritizing regeneration.*

James hadn't even realized he'd become airborne until he landed with a solid thump. He sat as his armor patched itself. The entire area was brighter than before—much brighter, despite the dirt and rock that rained around him. The expanded vision that came with his helmet confirmed his new situation.

Oh, wait. I'm outside. Huh. Funny.

He lay on the side of a huge crater that led into the cavern. Laena's monstrous form stood about fifty yards away and writhed in the remains of the underground prison.

The tower listed to the side. A deep, ominous groan filled the air, and the slow process of the entire structure toppling began. With a grunt, he leapt away from the crater before the building fell. The force of the impact hurled even more dirt into the air to form a decent-sized cloud. Huge chunks of the tower launched during the collision pounded into the earth. The liquid from the puddles splashed everywhere to create a sizzling, deadly rain. The strange light distortion from before had vanished.

Maximum adaptation to existing damage type already achieved, Whispy reported. *Initiating respiration filter due to local aerosolized toxic vapor exposure.*

"I wonder if she actually crushed herself," James muttered. "That would be a dumb ending." The holes in his armor had been repaired but some of the pain from the earlier attack lingered.

A black beam sliced through the rubble.

Laena burst from the piles of rock and crystal and bellowed in several voices at once. "Why won't you die?" she shrieked.

He shrugged. "My wife says I'm stubborn."

The Drow repeated her black-lightning attack. This time, he staggered but it only burned a few layers of armor off. His underlying wounds hadn't been fully healed, so the strike intensified his existing pain, but he'd felt far worse. She hadn't even severed his arm. *Amateur.*

Near maximum adaptation to attack type achieved, Whispy reported.

"I told you," he shouted. "I'm not the same man I once was. Fuck it. I might as well step it up, too. You already killed everyone and knocked the tower down. It's not like I can make the situation worse."

I don't want penetration, he thought. *I want maximum explosion. Exactly like that shit in Chile.*

Noted, Whispy responded. *Please note massive area damage guaranteed.*

That's the fucking idea. If I blow this whole place up at this point, it'll be an improvement.

"You will not win against me a second time, James Brownstone. I will not allow it."

"I didn't ask for your fucking permission."

Laena launched yet another black-lightning attack. It charred the top layer of the armor and the assault barely stung.

Maximum adaptation to attack type achieved, Whispy confirmed. *Kill the enemy.*

James planted both his feet firmly on the ground. Lines of bright green energy crackled across his blades. They increased in frequency and arced in front of him. A jerking, twisting curtain of green light grew.

"I will kill you and I will drink your soul," she declared. "I will ensure that your daughter suffers slowly and painfully before I drink hers as well. You will know agony that you've never experienced."

A massive blast erupted from the light curtain and rocketed toward the strange creature that had once been the beautiful Drow queen. The attack struck and a massive green shockwave shredded the land and the remains of the building, carrying debris as it expanded. The shockwave caught him and hurled him back. He landed hard and rolled several times.

Unhurt, he stood and admired his latest creation, a huge mushroom cloud. He waited as the fruits of his assault rained slowly around him. A few minutes ticked away until his newly dug crater came into view, free of Laena.

He scoffed. "Yeah, regenerate from that shit."

Recommend seek out large-scale tactical conflict for increased chance of adaptation, Whispy sent.

Nah, he thought. *Alison wanted me to do one thing. Kick Laena's ass, and I did. It's all up to her now. She can't always have Dad looking over her shoulder. We'll sit and wait until she sends someone to pick us up. That's the one thing you never learned. All those symbionts you've absorbed, and you can't portal.*

Irritation flooded his mind.

Increased tactical and regeneration capabilities necessitate genetic trade-offs that result in loss of capabilities considered less valuable given host general engagement strategy, Whispy sent. *This information was previously provided.*

Yeah, I know. I'm fucking with you. I don't like that portal shit anyway. It's creepier than flying. Maybe that's why it took Alison so long for hers. Whatever, I don't give a shit. I still have a nice F-350 at home to carry me around.

CHAPTER TWENTY-FIVE

Wide-eyed, Drae watched the destruction of the prison and James' final attack through a scrying window. She took several deep breaths and slowly raised her trembling hand. Utterly shaken, she grasped her wrist with her other hand and stood from her bench, the only permanent feature in the otherwise empty room.

"No," she murmured. "Some miscalculations were made, but this doesn't mean I've lost. Laena was simply a means to an end. I must remember that. I won't let myself be afraid of James or Alison Brownstone. I will soon be queen of the Drow, and they will be dead."

There was a light knock on the door.

"Come in," she called and smoothed her expression. Her subjects should see nothing but confidence. The battle was not yet won.

A Drow man entered and bowed his head. "My princess, the enemy army is routing our main force, and James Brownstone has defe—"

"I know," she snapped and her heart pounded. "I've already seen it. The prison is of no concern."

"Should we save our other forces?" he asked with hope in his voice.

"No. They will die, but they will still take some of the enemy with them." She took slow, measured breaths. "It is an acceptable loss. We will simply have to accelerate the rest of the plan. I wanted more time but it doesn't matter."

The man looked away. "My princess, I will follow you to the death, but don't we risk failure?"

Drae scoffed. "All plans risk failure. What ultimately separates the strong from the weak is that the strong don't let themselves be overwhelmed by failure. This is why Laena failed. She was weak in the end. Yes, admittedly, despite the artifact enhancement, empowerment rituals, and souls fed to Laena, she was more easily defeated than I anticipated." She sneered. "It's exactly as before. If she had been a strong queen, this wouldn't have happened. She would still reign and James Brownstone would be another dead man who dared to oppose her."

"I don't understand, Princess Drae. Why would you give her the power? You've made it clear to all of us that you are to be queen. None of us have questioned it, but—"

"Don't you see? She was an arrogant fool so it was easy to use her." She flicked her wrist dismissively. "None of the magic I had fed into her was stable. She would be able to live a few hours at most and rampage, drawing the attention of the other princesses' forces and allowing our army to wait while they depleted themselves defeating the dangerous monster that slew the Queenslayer or any others who dared to oppose her. She was my instrument of fear, nothing more."

She resisted the urge to grind her jaw. That had been the plan, at least. She'd studied the earlier battle between James Brownstone and the queen and learned everything she could possibly know about the limits of his abilities. She had anticipated that Alison would call upon her father and hoped to use the knowledge of his death at the hands of the enhanced Laena to crush her spirit and break her army. How had it all gone so wrong?

No. I will win. I can't fail against that half-breed and that weakling. They will die.

"Laena's death changes nothing!" she bellowed. She looked at her scrying window. "James Brownstone has not even moved. Either he's too weak to fight on or there is a reason why he's not being brought to reinforce the half-breed and her allies. We simply need more time for our final plan." She pointed at the man. "Tell everyone to prepare for the ritual. It's time I accept what is mine."

I will not fail. I am the Princess of the Deepest Night and I will become queen.

CHAPTER TWENTY-SIX

Alison and Rasila flew side by side. They maintained a modest speed so as to not outpace their forces below. They had routed Drae's first army in short order and left a small group to take care of the survivors while the princesses led their forces to engage the other enemy warriors. The allied army had rushed toward the other side of the city, where the rest of Drae's forces had deployed. Unfortunately, their prison reinforcements couldn't portal to them because of the disruption spells that choked most of the city. Alison suspected they'd have to go block by block to scour for artifacts when everything was over, but a quick visual check from the air confirmed additional friendly warriors were closing on their position.

The final battle was close but bizarrely, from what she could see in the distance, the enemy army waited patiently for their arrival.

I'm lucky these people are still stuck in a very old-school way of thinking. Technomagic's beginning to be something on Earth, but if they'd spent more time on that kind of thing instead of hiring mercenaries, this could have been even worse. Or maybe we're lucky that they wanted to terrorize this city but not completely obliterate it.

A few strategic-level spells could easily have wiped this place off the map. I can't be sure anymore that Drae even cares about the Great Treaty.

"She attacked the city," Alison commented, wanting Rasila's input, "but she kept it small-scale. She could have simply opened with a massive aerial bombardment."

"There's terrorizing people into obeying you and then there is pushing them to destroy you," the other princess replied. "Drae is smart enough to know how closely she can challenge that line."

She frowned. "You make it sound like something you might do."

"No. I don't judge any Drow for killing a Drow in a challenge. We're a warrior people. But Drae's a coward who refuses to face any of us while she slaughters non-warriors. Even Laena fought her own battles. She was only despised because she killed so many unnecessarily. The Drow aren't humans. We don't have billions to replace us when one dies. A death isn't a tragedy but it should be worth something."

"It doesn't matter if its thousands or billions," she countered. "A life is a life."

"Perhaps, but I still don't understand what this has to do with Laena," Rasila complained. "Drae would destroy us and then turn the throne over to her? I dislike her having successfully deceived us, but I'll feel better about it once she's dead."

"There's something we're missing, but it doesn't matter

anyway. I wonder if Dad's already killed her. It might be over quickly if she says something to piss him off, and Laena's not exactly the kind of woman who was good at holding her tongue."

Rasila gave her a sidelong glance and some of the earlier irritation faded from her face. "You didn't even consider the possibility that he might lose? Undoubtedly, Drae would have provided some kind of artifact or method to increase her power."

"Anything's possible but no, there's no way Dad would lose to her." She shrugged. After a moment, she narrowed her eyes and gestured to a small army of Zain that loped down a connecting avenue in a tightly packed cluster like a hungry pack of land piranhas. Another contingent of mercenaries rushed from the opposite side.

Disdain returned to Rasila's face. "All those complaints about human interference and she's reduced to using such creatures. I'm almost honored that she's so afraid of us that she brought them in. She wouldn't have bothered if she thought she could win without them."

Alison stopped moving forward and hovered in place. She raised her hand to her mouth and drew on a few strands of magic. "Everyone, hold position!" Her voice came out as a thunderous bellow. The allied army stopped moving within seconds.

Rasila halted, a curious look on her face. "Our people can handle Zain."

"All it takes is a lucky swipe to hurt or kill someone," she argued. "And that means we have one fewer warrior to face Drae's army. This can't be a draw. We need to beat her so badly that no one will ever think about supporting her or even her memory." A wicked grin appeared on her face. "And she's made a big, bold show here. She's tried to show her power by terrorizing people." She gestured toward one of the Zain armies. "Maybe some other princesses should remind everyone that Drae's not the only one they need to be afraid of."

She wasn't comforted by her companion's eager grin, even if she supported her plan.

"What do you intend, Alison?"

"With our people not moving and everyone else out of the area, it means we can really let loose," she explained and pointed to an intersection. The two mercenary groups would reach it soon. It was obvious they intended to merge and attack the allied force.

"A joint explosive spell?" Rasila suggested.

Alison shook her head. "It's flashy but it's too impersonal."

The woman laughed. "Do you want it to sing to the enemy before it destroys them?"

"No." She licked her lips. "I think we need something that takes us right in there. That way, when people talk about this battle later, they'll want to talk about that. It's dramatic. Remember that tactic I discussed with you a few weeks ago?"

Understanding dawned on her companion's face. "Ah. We didn't have a chance to practice it. If we don't properly direct the energy, we stand a good chance of killing one another." She laughed. "That would be deliciously ironic—our deaths without Drae ever lifting a finger."

"I'm sure you can handle it." Alison glided forward and raised her hands. Bands of light and shadow condensed around her hands and arms. "And I know I can."

Rasila cackled. "Ah, yes, yes, yes. This is what I dreamed of. Fighting at your side, obliterating our enemies, and showing them the true power of a Drow princess." She raised her arms. Bands and strings of shadow swirled around her hands and arms.

Both princesses continued their slow advance while the magic collected. The cacophonous screeches of the Zain army sounded like something from a horror movie, but they were definitely about to turn the tables.

This is real. Everyone else on Oriceran stood on the outside and let this happen. Does that mean they don't care or were they confident it would be taken care of? Maybe in the end, despite everyone not wanting the Brownstones involved, they knew we would step in. No one likes the messy way we do things, but they don't mind our results. We might as well give the public what they want.

"We'll attack when they're in the intersection," she explained. "You take left and I'll take right. Get ready."

Rasila's smile gave way to a clenched jaw. Even a Drow princess on Oriceran could only channel so much magical energy without strain. Her arms had vanished completely under the thick purple-tinged shadows. Alison's concentrated magic, in contrast, represented her dual-nature in bright white bands interspersed with the dark lines of shadow.

The front of the mercenary ranks entered the target zone.

"Let them have it!" Alison screamed. Both princesses rocketed to the center of the intersection, their arms outstretched. She spun to her side so her back was to the other woman's.

So you thought you could scare me away, Drae? You don't know how Brownstones think. The more you try to scare us away, the more pissed off we become.

They pounded the magic into the ground and released their pent energy. Huge arcs of dark power surged away from the impact point and together, formed a roaring nova of destruction. The attack obliterated the Zain and ripped chunks out of the road surface. The wave of death continued to expand, shattered several smaller buildings nearby, and felled a surviving crystal tower.

The princesses stood. Thick dust all around obscured their vision. Silence captured the entire area. No screech, or growl, or cheer sounded. They waited as the light winds cleared the air.

They stood in the center of what had once been the Zain army, now nothing more than a blasted pile of charred meat. Although the force of the spell had damaged the top layer of the road and the ground, the directional discharge had prevented a deep crater from forming. Massive rhythmic thudding killed the silence. The allied army sprinted toward the intersection.

Alison didn't move. She waited as their warriors moved closer. They slowed and stopped and the individual members looked in stunned amazement at the destruction that two princesses combining their power could wreak.

A bloodied Hana emerged from the crowd. Her bright tails provided a stark contrast to the dark armor and skin of most of the army. "Damn, now I feel like a loser." She smirked at Mason. "This brings new meaning to that saying, 'Happy wife, happy life.'"

He snickered and shrugged.

Rasila laughed. "It's not enough to have power. One must have the opportunity to use it."

Alison stared at her hands. Would it be enough? She'd destroyed the Zain because she knew she couldn't reason with them, but she also hoped the display might convince the final Drow army to surrender. Though they lay a half-mile away, they had to be watching. They had to know how easily two Drow princesses had annihilated their enemy. Perhaps they believed in Drae's power more.

"Fear the Princess of the Shadow Forged and the Princess of the Endless Shadow!" bellowed a Drow from the center of the crowd. The rest of the army joined the cheer before they roared a joint shout of triumph.

Rasila leaned close to her to whisper, although with all the shouting, it was probably unnecessary. "Let's finish this. It doesn't end until she's dead. We need to do this for everyone who has suffered through her machinations."

"I agree." She turned quickly.

A spell exploded in the sky in the distance, writing out a glowing sentence in Drow.

LAENA IS DEFEATED. THE QUEENSLAYER HAS TRIUMPHED.

She grinned. "Thanks, Dad, and thanks whoever thought to send the message that way." She inclined her head down the road. "Now, even Drae knows her plan has failed. You're right, Rasila. It's time to finish this."

CHAPTER TWENTY-SEVEN

The allied army didn't hurry toward the waiting forces. If the enemy had ceased their attack, there was no reason to rush. Alison had momentum and power on her side. Even though her dad wouldn't be involved, it was enough that some of Drae's warriors might suspect that he would be. Drae might even surrender with her main army crushed and her plan thwarted.

A slow approach after such an impressive display of power would give their adversaries more time to consider whether they wanted to be on the receiving end of such an attack. They had no reason to suspect that she wanted to minimize Drow casualties, but at the same time, she would do whatever she could to stop the battle. She would need to punish people later for attacking the city, but she would concentrate on Drow leaders among the enemy army.

The enemy stood arranged in neat little lines like they were ready for a parade. They didn't move or call out as the allied army advanced, the two princesses flying overhead. Alison admired their discipline. She wasn't so sure she could remain so calm after seeing someone blow monsters up with such ease.

She waited until they were about fifty yards away and called. "Hold position!" Her warriors froze in place. They had their arms up and wielded weapons of shadow or physical magical swords. They would fight and die at her command, but if she did everything correctly, they wouldn't have to do either.

It's time for a little theatricality. Who would have thought those plays in school would have helped in this kind of situation?

There was one last chance to avoid more bloodshed, but it depended on Drae's sense of self-preservation. A woman that intelligent had to realize she was already outclassed.

"I am Alison Brownstone," she shouted. "Princess of the Shadow Forged, and I'm here with Rasila, Princess of the Endless Shadow. Drae, Princess of the Deepest Night, our forces have destroyed your other army. Whatever scheme you had to release Laena has failed. Your Zain mercenaries are dust. Now, if you want to claim the right to ascend the throne, you can't hide behind other Drow or mercenaries. Come and face us. Maybe you never wanted the throne. Isn't that why you conspired to release Laena?"

A little taunt might expedite things. Anything she could do to undermine their adversary in front of the other Drow couldn't hurt, either.

A wide building near the rear of the army exploded. A column of purple-tinged shadow hurtled into the air. A single form rose into the sky from the ruins of the burning debris.

Six huge shadow wings extended from Drae's body,

each twice as long as Alison's standard wing. A dark purple aura covered her, and her eyes had turned solid black. She floated above her warriors, an almost serene look on her face.

Okay, she looks a little different, but that doesn't mean anything. Still, I sense that she won't simply surrender after that entrance.

"Congratulations, Alison and Rasila," Drae said glibly. "You've done me a favor. I must thank you for your service."

Alison chuckled. "What? You were really hoping we'd destroy your mercenaries and your army?"

"You disposed of Laena," she explained. "You thought I wanted to bring her back? No, she was merely a tool to use against you, and it accomplished exactly what I needed—delays and splitting your forces. Her early death doesn't bother me. She would have died eventually anyway, but this minimizes further losses to our people."

Damn. She played us, after all.

Rasila scoffed so loudly it echoed among the nearby buildings. "Losses to our people? You attacked this city indiscriminately. You have killed Drow for no reason except your own arrogance and avarice."

"I will not be lectured by a weak princess who would subordinate herself to a half-human." Drae sneered. "She's an outsider and she's brought outsiders. Everything I've done is to keep the Drow strong."

Alison uttered a harsh laugh. "Are you kidding me?" She kept her voice amplified so everyone below could hear clearly. "You filled a Drow city with Zain. You brought in non-Drow to murder Drow, and you act superior because

I'm half-human and I brought in a few of my friends? You're worse than a coward and a hypocrite. You're an idiot and you're a disgrace to Drow princesses and the Drow people. I'm giving you one last chance to stop this before I send you to join Laena on the Brownstone Death Express."

Drae clenched her teeth. Despite the huge numbers of people below, no one spoke a single word.

"You will not yield to me?" she demanded and broke the silence.

"I'll only yield when I'm dead," she insisted.

"I will not serve a coward." Rasila glared at Drae. "And you are the worst kind of coward."

"The Drow will only survive with true strength!" the woman shouted and gesticulated widely at the crowd. "Only I will provide that strength. The Guardians were weak, which is why I had them killed and why I killed the last few myself. And, yes, I employed certain stratagems and misdirection for my goals, but intelligence and misleading the enemy is part of strength. Laena failed her people, so I gave her one last chance to serve them, but it's too late. You two don't understand that I've achieved what I set out to do. You lack vision, which is why neither of you should be queen." She inclined her head toward her wings. "You don't seem surprised. I think it's because you don't understand the implications. You don't appreciate what all my careful planning has achieved. You're fools."

Alison gave her most dismissive shrug. "From what I can tell, all your careful planning has achieved nothing more than many dead Drow and Zain. Who needs a queen who killed more of her own people than an invader? The

Drow are people, not toys to be tossed aside when you're having a tantrum."

The purple aura around Drae flared. "The Shadow Forged bloodline is wasted. The wish passed down through that bloodline was wasted. You disgust me, human."

"Is that what this is about?" Her gaze flicked to Rasila. The other princess had said similar things in the past, although she had long since changed her opinion. "Too damned bad. That doesn't justify anything you've done."

"As queen, I originally intended to use the rituals to transfer the path of the wish," Drae explained. "I still will once I am queen, but it's not as important now."

"Why is that?"

"Because I have found a better solution. I discovered a way to channel some of the energy of a wish into me, even if it's not a true wish." Drae spread her arms. "Every sacrifice that has occurred today has not been wasted. The life-force expended has passed into me. I'm far more powerful than any Drow here."

Rasila trembled with barely concealed rage. "You sacrificed our own people for your power? You have become Laena." She spat on the soil at her feet. "You disgust me. My only regret is that I can't kill you slowly."

Drae laughed. "I've become Laena?"

"Yes!"

"No! I have exceeded her. I will become the strongest queen the Drow have ever known."

Alison sighed and shook her head. "Do you think the other races will tolerate what you've admitted to? Even if you managed to win against us, King Oriceran might understand the implications of a queen who is willing to empower herself by killing her own people. It's not that hard to see how you might turn to other races as sources for power. If we don't stop you here, you all but guarantee another war. I'm very sure whatever rituals you used are probably on the list of forbidden magic."

"Your words are nothing but nonsense from a weakling," Drae countered. "You speak of sacrifice? What of the warriors who have died fighting in your name?"

"They choose to fight and die, and I fight alongside them and risk my own life. I don't kill them to make myself stronger while I hide far from the battle. The funny thing is, if you weren't such a damned coward, you might have been able to defeat Rasila's army before I arrived. But all you care about is yourself, and now we're here and your other army is gone." She gestured toward Drae but spoke to the crowd. "Is this who you will serve? A woman who thinks of you as nothing more than fuel for her power? A woman who would slaughter Drow with mercenaries? A woman who sat, hiding, while loyal Drow warriors died?"

Rasila nodded approvingly at the speech and a calm expression settled on her face.

Angry shouts erupted from the enemy army.

"All loyal subjects should be willing to die for their queen," Drae thundered. "The queen is the heart of the Drow, and I will soon be queen. No, I am queen. I have seized the power and you will recognize my authority."

Alison smirked. "The last queen with that kind of attitude had a little problem getting her ass kicked by a Brownstone."

Drae scoffed. "And will you run to your father, Alison?

Are you nothing more than a child who trusts a parent to save them?"

"No. I specifically told my dad to stay out of this fight. And I want everyone else to stay out of this fight, too. There are three Drow princesses left, and if this is about proving strength, we should prove our own strength." She pointed at her adversary. "If you want to be queen, let's settle it right here. No armies. No mercenaries. No nine-tailed foxes with swords. Only you, me and Rasila."

The corners of Drae's mouth curled in a sneer. "Do you intend to aid this farce, Rasila? It wasn't that long ago you claimed you should be queen."

"You don't have to worry about me, Drae," the other princess responded cheerfully. "I'll deal with Alison in my own way after you're dead."

"Drae, Princess of the Deepest Night." Alison spoke in a cold and formal tone. "We challenge you. Do you accept our challenge, or are you the coward everyone knows you are?"

Every Drow below thrust their fists into the air. "Challenge!" they shouted and backed away to provide more room for the fight.

"I won't spare you," Drae explained. "I will kill you and Rasila and then I will kill your father, your mother, your infant brother, and anyone you ever cared for. I will leave the Brownstone name a symbol of pathetic weakness and grandiose posturing for millennia. I'll even kill the dog in your father's house."

"Never threaten a Brownstone dog." She grinned. "To quote something my mother once said, 'What? Will you talk me to death?'" She floated back and layered more shields.

"I've wanted to kill you for a long time, Drae," Rasila admitted. "But I will destroy you mostly because you would lead our people to ruin."

Alison increased altitude but kept her attention on Drae. "I'm not doing this for myself. I'm doing this for all those people you threatened and all those you've already killed, the ones I couldn't save. Including Miar. You'll die, Drae, and your name will last in history as an example of a crazy bitch whose reach exceeded her grasp. Let's do this, Rasila, for Miar."

In answer, the other princess brought her hand back. Swirling shadows gathered in it. "For Miar!"

CHAPTER TWENTY-EIGHT

Rasila launched her gathered shadows toward Drae. The spell burst into a shower of blue-black sparks that pelted the purple aura. Alison decided to open her attacks with several rapid light orbs. The bright spells exploded against the other woman with loud pops. They forced her back a few yards but her aura didn't dim and her frown remained fixed on her face.

Nice opener, she thought.

Drae soared toward Rasila and the light around her hands glowed brighter. Her target dropped, avoided the sweep of the other princess' hand, and flew away. Alison circled them and maintained a fast speed but focused more of her magic into her constant stream of attacks, mostly orbs and crescents. She was so practiced with them that she could shove them out in an almost staccato rhythm.

Rasila and I spent considerable time fighting before we got here and Drae's all souped-up on souls, but she's also overconfident. From everything Rasila's told me, she never was the best fighter. We can win this. We simply have to make her screw up.

Drae pursued Rasila and caught up quickly. Her turning and acceleration were noticeably faster than either of the challengers. The extra shadow wings weren't for show. It wasn't impossible for Alison to summon more, but in her experience, the massive increase in required magical energy wasn't worth the trade-off. The other Drow didn't seem to strain at all.

I doubt we can simply run her out of magic, not on Oriceran, but that doesn't mean she has infinite shields.

She shoved out several more orbs. They exploded around the princess but her aura remained strong.

Rasila extended a shadow blade and swung at her pursuer but the blade simply bounced off Drae. She retaliated and shoved her energy-wreathed palm against her attacker's chest. A huge shockwave surged from the point of contact and Rasila plummeted into a free fall that cracked the hard surface of the road below on impact. Drae tumbled for a few seconds with the force of her attack before she righted herself.

Alison alternated between light orbs and shadow crescents now in an attempt to whittle away her opponent's defenses. With her enemy's current extra power, she might not be able to win a direct exchange of firepower, but no matter how empowered Drae was, it was still two princesses against one.

We will win this.

Rasila pushed off the ground and wiped the blood from her mouth. Shadows began to fill her wounds, including the deep burn in her chest that had destroyed her armor and the clothes beneath. She growled with anger and dark lines of energy crackled around her.

"Is this your much-vaunted power?" she taunted. "I'm not impressed by one lucky blow, Drae. I only hope I'm the one who strikes the fatal wound. I'll show you real power, you cowardly imposter princess."

"This is futile," Drae insisted. She rushed Alison, who avoided her deadly touch with a quick roll. "Do you not understand? You can't win against this kind of power." She abandoned her direct assault and thrust her palms out to fire a stream of purple-tinged orbs that burst into numerous vicious shadow missiles.

Alison barrel-rolled to avoid the attacks and flung a few crescents behind her at the princess. Out of the corner of her eye, she could see Rasila continuing to gather energy.

I need to give her more time. If she wants to be the one to kill Drae, that's fine with me.

She changed direction abruptly and jerked almost perpendicular from her original course. Another quick change altered her trajectory toward Drae who swayed to keep herself in motion as she maintained her fire. The shadow orbs detonated around Alison and stung and weakened her shields. She realized that a direct hit might be enough to knock her out of the sky and held back her own assault while she concentrated on evading the barrage.

Rasila drew her arm back. The energy flowed over her and formed into a pitch-black spear. She threw the weapon and it soared toward Drae, its speed increasing as it drew closer.

That's right. Kill the bitch.

Drae spun to face Rasila and Alison resumed her attack, this time with shadow crescents. The spear ripped through the purple protective aura and the princess' chest to gouge out a huge chunk. Blood splattered from the wound but immediately, shadows filled it. She continued her attacks, but their adversary only flinched as the crescents struck home and in some cases, sliced into her body. Drae dropped toward Rasila and her arm transformed into a dark tentacle.

"You can't defeat me," she screamed. "You're less than worthless. You dare call me an imposter?"

Alison switched to rapid-firing light orbs by alternating her palms in an attempt to distract her, but the woman continued to ignore the missiles, even when they exploded against her and burned her exposed flesh.

This is nothing. A Brownstone who can't fight with a few injuries doesn't deserve to be called a Brownstone.

Rasila conjured a shadow blade and set her feet, ready to receive the charge.

Her opponent's tentacle whipped out. She tried to parry the blow, but the appendage slipped under the blade and struck her shoulder and she screamed when it tore her arm off.

"Rasila!" Alison shouted.

Drae laughed. She impaled the princess through the abdomen before she yanked her tentacle out and wound it around her neck. "I am your queen, and you will obey me." She battered her opponent's body repeatedly against the ground before she flung it aside.

The wounded princess moaned. Her eyes fluttered and her blood pooled beneath her. Mason, Zana, and several other Drow rushed toward her.

Drae turned toward her other adversary. "Don't you

see, half-breed? Don't you see the power I wield? I studied everything that went wrong before very carefully. I understood why Laena lost, and I learned how to adapt to it. I know how to channel the power she used without becoming a monster and how to avoid burning myself out."

Alison floated in place, her jaw clenched and her heart pounding. She wasn't about to lose another friend, and she wasn't about to let an insane, murderous woman become queen of the Drow. She released her wings and let herself drop to land on one knee.

"That's right, bend your knee to me, Princess of the Shadow Forged," Drae taunted. The aura around her grew brighter. "You can't win against your queen. Come here and kiss my feet. Beg for my forgiveness, and I promise you that I'll spare the life of your friends."

Alison readied her arm and began to yell. She dropped her shields and drew on her light and shadow magic. A bright lance covered with dark spirals grew from her hand.

So many people helped me become who I am. Mom, Dad. So many friends helped me. Izzie, Lily, Hana, Miar. There were so many people I couldn't save through my own power. Tanner, Abner.

My first mother died. If I weren't weak at the time, I might have been able to save her myself, or I could have convinced her to use the wish to save herself.

In that moment, she realized something important. Even though her AMDS had long since been cured, there was a small part that still affected her mind, the part that told her to never truly go one hundred percent and always hold some small measure of energy back. She took that part of her mind and shoved it into the abyss. She was on

Oriceran, the planet of magic, and she would drink that magic to fuel her attack and ignore anything other than the power. Pain and fear were irrelevant. Drae needed to be destroyed.

It's my turn to protect everyone.

"No more!" Alison shouted. "I will not lose any more people to evil bitches like you." The spear grew longer and brighter while the dark bands swallowed more of their light. "I am Alison Brownstone, Princess of the Shadow Forged and future queen of the Drow, and you're nothing more than a pretender to the throne."

A soft female voice whispered in her ear, a voice she hadn't heard since she used the wish—that of her birth mother. "I'm proud of you, Alison. Show her true power."

She screamed with rage and purpose and threw the spear. Drae thrust her arms forward to thicken her defenses even more. The spear lanced completely through her protective aura and into her chest. A huge blinding explosion consumed the princess and the force of the blast hurled Alison off her feet.

Unconsciousness fought to overwhelm her and she focused on the sky to resist it. A shadow fell over her.

"If you're Drae, kill me without any taunts," she muttered. "I can't take more of your obnoxious-ass posturing."

Mason leaned over and scooped her into his arms. He inclined his head to the side and she forced herself to look in that direction. There was a decent-sized crater and no sign of Drae. He held her arm up. The gathered Drow thrust their fists up and roared.

Her breath caught. "Rasila!" She jerked her head toward

her friend. The wounded princess lay on her back. Dark shadows covered half her body and her eyes were closed. Several Drow knelt beside her and streams of shadow flowed from their hands. Some chanted with their hands placed directly on her body.

"She's stable, A," he explained. "They'll even be able to reattach her arm."

"It's over." She stared stupidly at him. "We won."

"Yeah, A. You won." He smiled and kissed her forehead.

CHAPTER TWENTY-NINE

Rasila groaned, her back propped against a wall in a small building near the sight of the battle. Her wounds had been healed—including, as Mason predicted, her arm reattached—but she was pale and her breathing was weak.

Alison knelt beside her friend. "You've looked better."

"I knew I was right to put my trust in you," the princess responded. "If you weren't there, I would have been defeated and she would have killed me." She tried to stand but wavered on her feet. "She would be queen of the Drow."

Alison stood quickly, caught her, and helped her to sit. "Take it easy. Even Drow princesses can only take so much punishment."

"As you might have suspected, events after the fight aren't clear in my mind." Rasila frowned. "How long has it been?"

"Only about an hour."

"And what's going on?"

"Drae's warriors all pledged loyalty to me," she explained. "Everyone's now out searching the city for stray Zain or wounded. I think the problem with many of the elites is they forget that not every Drow is as tough as them. We'll worry about coordinating repairs later."

"You didn't order the other warriors imprisoned?" The woman sounded surprised.

"They pledged their loyalty and enough Drow have died today. I might not be as great at Drow politics as you, but I do realize that a princess totally kicking the ass of a woman who had enhanced herself with that kind of magic is enough to demonstrate to everyone who's strong and who's not." She shrugged, a merry smile on her face. "We'll find out who was in charge later. People have to pay for the attack on the city, but I want the commanders, not simply the people who were swept up in it."

Zana entered and bowed her head. "I apologize for the interruption, my princesses. A Light Elf has come. He claims to represent the king."

"Avrik," Rasila muttered. "Of course he'd come."

Alison nodded at Zana. "Let him in."

The Light Elf stepped in a moment later, dressed in finery more appropriate for a palace ball than a battlefield. His gaze flicked around the room. He took everything in with a faint look of disdain.

"Is your war over?" he asked and sounded impatient.

"Wow, no small talk first?" Alison asked. "At least buy a girl dinner first." She stood and dusted her hands off on her pants. "Not even a little congrats?"

Avrik narrowed his eyes. "We have examined the magical residues both here and at the prison. Drae used magic specifically prohibited in the Great Treaty. This is a serious matter and it is not something we can ignore as purely internal to the Drow. Nor can we ignore James Brownstone's involvement."

She folded her arms. "I've read the Great Treaty, you know. It was something we had to study at school. Do you know what it doesn't say?"

"What?" Avrik snapped.

"Thou shall not offend a Brownstone." She shrugged. "If it weren't for my dad, some super-enhanced soul-sucking Laena monster would be on the rampage right now. If you really want to lodge a big complaint, go ahead, but I suspect King Oriceran will probably want to let this go."

The elf's nostrils flared. "That doesn't mean we can ignore everything else that has happened."

"Oh? What's the plan? Execute the perpetrators? Send them to Trevilsom? The World in Between?" Alison lowered her arms and cracked her knuckles. "If you weren't watching, I blew the main woman responsible for using forbidden magic away, and my dad did the same to the other one. Drow are simple, in a way. Kick their asses and they start listening to you."

"And she has those who likely aided her," he challenged. "What of them?"

"Once things settle, we'll look into it. If they were coerced, that's one thing. If they weren't, Trevilsom will have a few new Drow prisoners who can think about what it means to aid people in using forbidden magic."

"You'd surrender them that easily?" Avrik sounded dubious.

"I don't trust any Drow who would use that kind of magic," she insisted. "That's not something I'll tolerate."

"That's not good enough. An example needs to be made. There have been far too many mockeries of the treaty since the gates reopened." He scoffed. "We've been able to ignore many since they technically happened on Earth, but this isn't the same situation."

Alison raised her brow. "Are you kidding me right now?"

He raised his chin and went full haughty Light Elf on her. "If the Drow can't control themselves, maybe someone else should."

She squared her shoulders and strode over to him until she was only six inches away. He seemed unperturbed and she locked gazes with him. It was time to channel her inner queen. "Let me make this shit very, very, very clear. Many Drow suffered because of Drae, and she's been destroyed because of it. I killed her. My people won't suffer now because someone else thinks they need to make a show. We had problems here, and we resolved them. Not only did we resolve them, but we kept them contained in our territory."

She jabbed a finger in his chest. "Now, unless you want this to become a bigger problem, you'll back the fuck off. Everything I know about King Oriceran suggests that he wouldn't want unnecessary trouble, so I think this is merely middle-manager angling for promotion garbage. And by the way, we Brownstones haven't forgotten that Laena had non-Drow help during that whole adoption crap. Now, ask yourself, Avrik—do you really want to go up against the Brownstones when they're already pissed off?"

Rasila laughed. "Yes, Alison! Perfect, my queen."

Avrik licked his lips and stepped away, and uncertainty replaced the haughtiness. "My understanding is that certain procedures are still necessary before you become queen."

"The queen situation will be resolved soon enough and without any further violence," Alison explained.

He sighed. "As long as the new queen agrees to publicly uphold the treaty and hand over any relevant offenders to Trevilsom, I don't see a reason to press the matter."

She gave him a cold smile. "I'm glad you can be reasonable. We'll be in touch."

The elf nodded politely and stepped out of the room.

Rasila smiled. "I would get on my knee to pledge my loyalty, my queen, but I need a little more rest first."

Alison shook her head. "That won't be necessary."

The woman's expression fell. "You can't possibly be willing to leave your people after all you have done. I wish to serve you, not be a shadow of you."

"No, it's not that." She tapped her forehead. "I thought of a better idea, a way to leverage both our talents and the strength of Earth and Oriceran. You've talked about looking to the future, and that's exactly what I plan to do."

CHAPTER THIRTY

I t felt entirely silly to be decked out in an abundance of jewels and an elaborate, low-cut magical gown that constantly changed shades as the light fell on her in different ways. There were also the ridiculous open-toed high-heeled boots covered in an elaborate embroidery of various dark flowers. Alison had barely listened as the woman who helped her dress waxed on and on about the ancient meaning of the flowers. The only thing that made it tolerable was Rasila being forced into a similar outfit beside her. Unfortunately, the sly smile on the other woman's face suggested that it appealed to her personal sense of fashion. It definitely wasn't business casual.

The princesses paced slowly over a blood-red carpet. It was night, with only the stars and the twin moons to provide any light. On either side, thousands of people stood watching them. Near the front, a smattering of non-Drow filled the rows, including most of Brownstone Security and other representatives from all over Oriceran, including Avrik. Several Earth ambassadors were present, as was Senator Johnstone, but mercifully, they let the ancient man have a seat. Hana gave Alison a thumbs-up and winked as she passed. Tahir rolled his eyes at his fiancée.

Low, melodic chanting filled the air from a choir near the front, accompanied by the occasional loud gong. The two princesses walked forward toward a pit of dark sand in front of the carpet. A lone woman in a bright white robe stood there, a Drow priestess so wizened she made Myna look young. The priestess held the horned crown of the Drow queen.

The measured pace of the approach made the walk seem like forever. Alison and Rasila finally arrived and stood, their backs straight, as two Drow approached in ornate ceremonial armor. Both held glowing daggers. They sliced through the back of their boots and stepped away. It was all part of the ritual.

The women kicked their boots off and entered the sand pit, the sand cold against their bare feet. The chanting and gongs ceased.

The priestess held the crown in front of her with both hands. "Let it be witnessed," she called and her voice boomed. "Queen Laena has perished. The Guardians have perished. Two rightful heirs to the throne stand before me, Alison, Princess of the Shadow Forged and Rasila, Princess of the Endless Shadow. They have proven their strength and wisdom." She stepped closer to them. "In the chaos after the first defeat of Laena, there were questions about the future of our people, but now they are answered. A new tradition arises." She held the crown above her head. "Let the Drow recognize our two new queens. Queen

Alison and Queen Rasila. Their strength will guide our people. May their shadows always swallow the false light."

"Their strength will guide our people," the crowd chanted. "May their shadows always swallow the false light."

The princesses knelt. The priestess murmured a quick incantation. The crown glowed as she yanked on it with one hand to draw a matching crown from its form. The two armored Drow advanced and each took one to place them on the heads of the new queens.

Alison and Rasila turned and faced their crowd. "We are the Drow," they chanted, "and our strength will overwhelm all who oppose us."

Every Drow in the gathering thrust their fist into the sky and cheered.

Hana munched on a dark-green fruit Alison didn't recognize, the silver tray held lightly in her other hand. Both new queens had circulated for the past hour, chatting with different VIPs, and she had finally escaped to talk to her friends.

Drow and guests filled the massive palace chamber as they mingled, chatted, or occasionally selected food from the long tables on either end of the room. She was amused by the Drow party etiquette of not providing any chairs. While she'd experienced it a few times when she'd trained with them, she'd forgotten how they viewed even parties as a battlefield. A man or woman who needed a chair at a celebration was weak. She never did understand why they didn't care if they sat on the floor, though. Maybe it was simply a way to be lazier when they prepared for parties.

"This fruit tastes like popcorn," Hana exclaimed. "That's the real magic." She looked around. "Where did Mason go?"

"Oh, there was a gnome ambassador who wanted to show him something." Alison shrugged. She grimaced as she saw a handsome Wood Elf waving at her from across the room,

The fox glanced at him. "Is there a problem?"

"No, everyone's already decided that since there are new queens, it's time to start buttering us up for trade treaties and that kind of thing." She groaned.

"I still don't understand how this works." Her friend laughed. "But I was fairly drunk at the victory party when you explained it."

"It's simple. We're co-queens. I took the idea from something Mom said and a few articles she sent me. I read about the Roman Republic and consuls. They elected two people who alternated running things. The system had its issues, but the heart of the idea was to avoid concentrating power. In this case, the idea is for me to help lead the Drow into the future with the authority I've earned from defeating Drae, while Rasila can help to keep things stable with her knowledge of the politics and economics."

"And she's fine with it?" Hana raised an eyebrow. "How do you know she won't poison your wine?"

"She's happy about it. At first, she didn't like that I wanted her to become a co-queen, but I convinced her it was best for appearances' sake. The Guardians left a sour taste in everyone's mouth." She gestured with her gloved hand. "Right now, the Drow need leaders, not councils. I'll alternate between spending time on Earth and Oriceran."

"And the company?"

"I won't close it, but I might work fewer jobs myself."

The fox nodded. "They don't want their queen doing work?"

"No, it's not like that." She laughed. "If anything, me kicking ass on a regular basis only reinforces my authority. I merely can't rely on Rasila forever. I need to pull my weight in terms of governance, too. The Drow system is inefficient and a total mess. Laena ran many things directly through her sycophants, and the Guardians each had their own little fiefdoms of power they controlled. We need to set something up where we actually have people responsible for things who are not merely there because they can kiss queen ass well."

Tahir emerged from the crowd. "In other words, you'll reinvent the civil service bureaucracy?"

Alison winced. "It sounds bad when you say it like that."

Hana sidled over to him and wound an arm around his waist. "Think about it, babe. We're now friends with a queen."

"That's not a completely horrible thing," he observed with a faint smirk.

The Wood Elf ambassador wove between a few people and closed in on Alison.

She sighed. "Yeah, sorry guys, the queen needs to escape. Talk to you later."

Her friend grinned. "Run, my queen. Run!"

CHAPTER THIRTY-ONE

A few weeks later, Hana held a sheer white low-cut wedding dress against her body. "So, what do you think?"

She and Alison stood between long rows of hanging gowns, a sea of brightly colored satin, chiffon, and lace.

Alison pointed to the skirt. "It's a wedding dress with a micro-mini skirt." She kept her tone neutral but hoped her friend understood her point.

"I know, right?" The fox grinned. "I only need a bra that matches my skin tone, but I'm sure if I can't find what I want, one of the fine spellcasters I know can help me. I'll be the sexiest bitch at that wedding."

She shook her head. "I'm not sure this is the right choice."

Hana furrowed her brow in thought. She draped the dress over her arm and gestured to another one on the rack. The skirt extended farther, but the top made Alison question the limits of how deep a V-neck cut could go before the top was nothing more than a few scraps of fabric.

"I'm not sure about that one either," she said firmly.

The fox frowned. "Yeah, you're right. I'm as sexy as hell, but I don't have much up top and it's like cheating if I go too heavy in the push-up department."

Alison chuckled. "Not that I want you to choose that dress, but Tahir's already seen you naked."

"Oh, I'm talking about everyone else." Hana winked.

She sighed. "Hana, it's your wedding and your choice, but you might want to balance taste with a sense of being alluring. You're supposed to be a bride, not a showgirl."

The bride-to-be laughed. "You're the one who had a Vegas wedding." She gasped and clutched the dress close to her body. "Do you know what I only now realized? The Vegas comment made me think of something."

"You want to have your wedding in Vegas?" she ventured.

"No, no, no. Rasila said she'd come and you're coming. Do you realize what that means?"

"You'll have at least two Drow at your wedding?" She shrugged.

"I'll have royalty at my wedding." She squealed.

"You already knew us before and technically, we were royalty before, too."

The woman blew a raspberry. "But now, you're an actual poker hand. A pair of queens. That's a decent hand. You can't win at poker with a pair of princesses." She scoffed playfully.

Alison chuckled. "I'm still adjusting to this whole idea. It's weird, but I suppose it's not any weirder than when I found out I was a Drow princess at the age of fifteen. For now, I'll live my Earth life mostly the same. I merely have to make a few adjustments here and there."

"Like your Queen's Guard?" Hana inclined her head toward two Drow women who inspected gowns farther away. They wore dark suits instead of armor, but the combination of very dark smooth skin, white hair, and pointed ears still made them stand out among the mostly human clientele of the bridal shop.

"It'll make jobs easier," she reasoned. "They want to fight with me when I choose to participate and even said they'd be insulted if I took on dangerous jobs without letting them help."

Hana waved to the Drow. They nodded politely in response.

"You could retire, you know. Simply do the queen thing and relax otherwise."

She sighed. "I've thought about it, but I still owe Earth and all my friends and family here. Now that I'm the Dark Queen rather than the Dark Princess, things are different. That's not totally bad, either. Admittedly, they're more complicated, but it also means I can help more people, both on Earth and Oriceran."

Her companion pulled another dress off the rack and wiggled her eyebrows. "Huh? Huh?"

Alison scrubbed a hand down her face. "That's not even a dress, really. It's basically a white bustier. You might as well go to a lingerie shop."

The fox beamed happily. "I know. Isn't it great?"

In bed, Alison rolled onto her elbow. Mason lay beside her, reading his phone in the dark.

"It's been a few weeks," she began. "Are you still okay with all of this?"

He tossed his phone on the nightstand and faced her. "I'm still adjusting to the whole royal consort scenario, but since Laena didn't have much of a court culture, at least there aren't a group of Drow courtiers trying to backstab me or seduce you."

"Yet." She grinned.

Mason ruffled her hair. "I never thought I would marry a queen, but I can't really complain."

Her grin faded. "Since I'm queen, there's no chance now that they'll try to transfer the wish."

"But you don't have the wish anymore. You used it in DC to restore your sight."

"But my bloodline has it. If I have a daughter, she might inherit a wish."

He raised his eyebrow. "What are you saying?"

She placed a hand over his heart. "I'm not ready to have a kid right away, but I do kind of wonder about having one sooner rather than later. I keep thinking about the best time, but when is the best time? I already own my own business, and I've ascended to a throne. If she'll gain the wish, I'd prefer that some of it be decided before too much in the way of annoying court politics settle in."

Mason nodded slowly, uncertainty on his face. "How long are you thinking?"

"A couple of years, maybe?"

His expression brightened. "That soon?"

Alison scooted over and rested her head on his chest.

"With everything that happens to me, we'd better get going. If we wait too long, I might end up pregnant while fighting someone for the position of queen of the galaxy."

He kissed her and pulled away to look at her. "Alison Brownstone, Queen of the Galaxy. That has a nice to ring to it."

THE END

We hoped you enjoyed the conclusion to the series! If you're looking for more books in the Oriceran Universe, be sure to check out the newest series, Scions of Magic.

Keep an eye out for new novels with Leira, Correk, Yumfuck and maybe even Izzie. You never know and you definitely don't want to miss them!

Get sneak peeks, exclusive giveaways, behind the scenes content, and more.
PLUS you'll be notified of special **one day only fan pricing** on new releases.

Sign up today to get free stories.

CLICK HERE

or visit: https://marthacarr.com/read-free-stories/

If smart phones and GPS rule the world - why am I hunting a magic compass to save the planet?

Austin Detective Maggie Parker has seen some weird things in her day, but finding a surly gnome rooting through her garage beats all.

Her world is about to be turned upside down in a frantic search for 4 Elementals.

Each one has an artifact that can keep the Earth humming along, but they need her to unite them first.

Unless the forces against her get there first.

<u>**AVAILABLE ON AMAZON AND IN KINDLE UNLIMITED!**</u>

For Hire: Teachers for special school in Virginia countryside.

Must be able to handle teenagers with special abilities.

Cannot be afraid to discipline werewolves, wizards, elves and other assorted hormonal teens.

Apply at the School of Necessary Magic.

New decade, new year, new month and I recently turned 60. That can make me look at things differently. I keep having the thought that if I haven't managed to change something by now, maybe I should make peace with it.

I mean how many decades do I keep trying to *fix* something before I realize the trying to fix it may be the problem. It's one of those things that I wish I had really understood better when I was a lot younger. And if I had it would have turned my outward search for what would make me fit better in the world, to an inward one of asking, what do I want?

What I want is to be happy with what is, instead of yearning for more or different like it's a necessity. In the past few years I've written as fast as I can, days, nights and weekends, holding down a full-time corporate job, and then moving and building a house, and the death of a sister. This past year I added on starting a universe on my own and trying to expand my business into other areas, while traveling far and wide at least once a month, sometimes more. I even held my old mini author convention in my house... twice.

I wasn't giving myself a chance to take a breath and absorb everything that happened, good and bad. There was no time.

Somewhere around the end of the year I knew I needed to make some changes. It was probably that impending end of one decade for both me and the planet and the start of another. And there's been something about 60 that's put things into a different perspective. What does all this running around add up to? I noticed I kept looking over at authors doing less work and more play or even just sitting still and wishing I was them.

Well, why can't I be them? I have choices. First one was to sell the new universe to LMBPN, pull all the books and reintroduce them, plus some new ones as the new Terranavis Universe. The relaunch started last week and already I feel lighter, happier. The next one was to stop planning business trips and just be here in the dream house for now with the dogs and get to know the neighbors. I made gingerbread cookies this Christmas and put my name, address and phone number and delivered them to everyone on my street. I started getting texts from everyone. It worked like a charm and I've even had a few over for dinner already.

I've also been getting up early and heading to the gym – one day at a time. Even yoga has seemed tough, but the bar is low – it can only get better. That's the other thing that I'm really getting these days. This body is a loaner I'll have to give back at some point and how I treat it will play a part in how long I get to use it and how much use I get out of it. That has really hit home lately.

But I don't need to do any of it perfectly, or as well as it seems someone else is doing, or even great every single day. I just have to try and occasionally ask myself, *is this still what you want?* And then adapt, change and head out again. Happy New Year Everyone! More adventures to follow.

AUTHOR NOTES - MICHAEL ANDERLE

(THE FUTURE) JANUARY 9, 2020 (MACAU CHINA SAR)

Thank you for not only reading this book but the whole series!

When I first thought of Alison, she was the humanizing aspect of the story for James Brownstone.

He was (and still is) a man who gets the job done. He isn't handsome, he likes to keep things simple, and helping others isn't on the top of his to-do list.

But allowing a young girl to get herself into trouble isn't either.

Eventually, he takes the young girl in and adopts her. She changes his life for the better while they both figure out she is the potential queen of the Drow on Oriceran.

(*James can't keep his life simple to save it. Seriously? Your adopted daughter is royalty?*)

But, like all good fathers, you don't screw with his daughter. Ever. To help her out, he trains her like he would any Brownstone, and very much against her teenage wishes.

And like a Brownstone of his bloodline, she sets off on her own path and her own future.

She has the lineage of her Drow mom (remember how she goes down protecting her daughter and giving James the kiss of his lifetime?) Also, she is raised by Shay, who worries about the young girl who grew Shay's heart three sizes for sure.

I have a particular fondness for Alison, and I'm very glad you have enjoyed her stories. From her white hair to the attitude she showed in Brownstone book 01, Alison will always have a place next to Bethany Anne in my heart.

Great characters I'd love to know personally.

When I "met" Alison, she was a young and naïve girl. As we leave her stories, she is a capable and amazing woman. My, how time flies when you are having fun!

If you enjoyed these stories, we (LMBPN Publishing) have hundreds more for your consideration. Take a moment and check us out at http://www.LMBPN.com .

Macau, China SAR

Presently, I'm writing this from the Galaxy Hotel (room 32098) in Macau, China. I suspect some of the knowledge I've gained here will make it into future stories.

There are two important pieces of information to know about me and why Macau is interesting. First, I live on the Strip in Vegas (for a few more months. In the summer, we will be spending time in Cabo San Lucas as well.)

Second, Macau is the largest (by dollars gambled) gambling city in the world. I wanted to know how the gambling is different between the two countries / localities, and the answer is...

It really isn't so much.

Yes, Vegas has WAY more strange things going on the walkways ("Cover Timmie's eyes, MaryAnne!") but other than I can't read much of anything (except when they provide the translations, which they do for most of the major signs) and the currency exchange messes up my life (Really? 8 HK dollars to a US dollar makes 235...HK Dollars...equal to... I think my head just exploded.)

Oh, and in the Galaxy Hotel... Well, the Galaxy hotel shared area, which is HUGE.

It's interesting because unlike Vegas, Macau uses a shared casino concept here. The casino is in the center, and the hotels (Galaxy, JW Marriott, and others) have their buildings on the outside of the casino floor circle.

In Vegas, we assume the casino floor is under the hotel rooms. While technically they are not (too large a footprint to fit under the hotel), it feels like you are all part of the same building.

Except for the Four Seasons, which is part of Mandalay Bay complex.

Today we switch from the Galaxy over to the Four Seasons, which abuts the Venetian casino setup (and the Parisian.)

Talk about déjá vu! When riding into Macau, I saw a bus for the Venetian Macau, all in English, with the same typography / artwork as the Venetian in Las Vegas. I felt like I was in Vegas for a split second, and then I saw the road signs.

Nope, not in Vegas.

As a devout meatatarian (with honorary potatoes in the diet), eating here is very difficult for me.

One, I don't speak the language, so I can't easily ask questions about what is in the food. I personally love beef fried rice, as long as it has no vegetables and extra egg. Plus, I like hot oil.

They don't have pictures for taking out vegetables and "Noooo…vegetables…please…" doesn't work. They need me to man up and learn enough of the dialect to explain what I want.

Judith, God bless her, had me ask a Chinese waiter in Sydney to write down my order in Chinese. I used that slip of paper in Hong Kong to order my rice.

Just a note—many Chinese do not consider onion to be a vegetable.

So, I'm on the hunt for American restaurants or food. I tested a few places, including Urban Modern (JW Marriot), and I'm going back for breakfast as soon as I finish these author notes.

I tested the McDonald's here in the Galaxy hotel.

NOTE: They do not take credit cards at the counter.

The second time I went to McDonald's, I had cash. The food was something I could eat (sausage egg McMuffin and fries with a Coke.).

The hotdog place I tried? Let's just say the fries were delicious, but I don't want to relive the hotdog part.

I've learned that in other places around the world, my version of a hotdog is nothing like what they serve as hotdogs in the US. For one, I like an easy-to-bite hotdog, not one that POPs as you use significant jaw strength to cut through the casing.

I still don't know what the bun bread was made out of, but I wasn't expecting a really sweet bun.

Damn, here I am reliving the hotdog part.

That hotdog experience is going into a story, I promise you.

If you enjoyed these stories about Alison or any others (from any authors!), please consider taking a moment to review them. You are helping those authors help market their books, now and into the future.

I'll see you in the next series!

Ad Aeternitatem,

Michael Anderle

THE WITCHES OF PRESSLER STREET
THE ADVENTURES OF FINNEGAN
DRAGONBENDER
THE ADVENTURES OF MAGGIE PARKER

Other series:

THE LAST VAMPIRE
THE WITCH NEXT DOOR

OTHER BOOKS BY JUDITH BERENS

OTHER BOOKS BY MARTHA CARR

**JOIN THE ORICERAN UNIVERSE FAN GROUP ON
FACEBOOK!**